A Begonia for Miss Applebaum

Also by Paul Zindel

The Amazing and Death-Defying Diary
of Eugene Dingman

Confessions of a Teenage Baboon

The Effect of Gamma Rays
on Man-in-the-Moon Marigolds
(a play)

The Girl Who Wanted a Boy

Harry & Hortense at Hormone High

I Love My Mother
(a picture book, illustrated by John Melo)

I Never Loved Your Mind

Let Me Hear You Whisper
(a play, illustrated by Stephen Gammell)

My Darling, My Hamburger

Pardon Me, You're Stepping on My Eyeball!

The Pigman

The Pigman's Legacy

A Star for the Latecomer
(with Bonnie Zindel)

To Take a Dare
(with Crescent Dragonwagon)

The Undertaker's Gone Bananas

PAUL ZINDEL

A Begonia for Miss Applebaum

HARPER & ROW, PUBLISHERS
Grand Rapids, Philadelphia,
St. Louis, San Francisco,
London, Singapore, Sydney, Tokyo, Toronto
NEW YORK

A Begonia for Miss Applebaum

Printed in the United States of America. For information address Harper & Row Junior Books, 10 East 53rd Street, New York, N.Y. 10022.
Typography by Al Cetta
2 3 4 5 6 7 8 9 10

Library of Congress Cataloging-in-Publication Data
Zindel, Paul.
A begonia for Miss Applebaum.

"A Charlotte Zolotow book."
Summary: Discovering that their beloved former teacher Miss Applebaum is terminally ill, fifteen-year-old Henry and his friend Zelda accompany her on her excursions to the colorful parts of New York City and join her in confronting death with quiet courage.
[1. Teacher-student relationships—Fiction.
2. Death—Fiction. 3. New York (N.Y.)—Fiction]
I. Title.
PZ7.Z647Be 1989 [Fic] 88-11010
ISBN 0-06-026877-8
ISBN 0-06-026878-6 (lib. bdg.)

TO ANY KID WHO READS THIS:

Something terrible has happened. There are no lies in this book and nothing phony. We are writing it on an APPLE IIE during our computer class at high school while most of the other kids are playing Donkey Kong and Demon Attack. We have to tell the whole story because we thought what we were doing was right. Well, maybe it wasn't. Maybe we were very wrong. We still don't know. Maybe you will understand, and be able to help us. Please don't think we meant to hurt Miss Applebaum. Please don't think that at all.

Sincerely,

Henry and Zelda

A Begonia for Miss Applebaum

Chapter One

Well, you might as well know all about *me* and then you'll understand how Zelda and I got involved in what happened to Miss Applebaum. You probably never knew Miss Applebaum, but she was our 62-year-old biology teacher last year at Andrew Jackson High. Our nickname for Miss Applebaum was "The Shocker" because she loved to surprise her classes. In fact, the exact day we started to call Miss Applebaum "The Shocker" was when she brought in a Bloomingdale's gift box and opened it to reveal a dead cat. The cat was a weird-looking one with white-tipped paws and a black body. It wasn't that she had just scooped it up off 59th Street after a taxi had hit it, or anything like that. It was already embalmed and sealed in plastic. Miss Applebaum said dissecting a dead cat wasn't her idea of a good time, but it was part of the New York City Board of Education syllabus. She told us she put it in a gift box so all the kids in the class would know this cat had given a present of its life in order for us to learn about cat anatomy. She also believed the cat deserved the dignity of a name. We voted to call it Louis. She didn't allow smiling either when she demonstrated why the tabby was properly called

Louis and not Louisa. Actually, there are thousands of things Zelda and I have to tell you about Miss Applebaum, but you'd better know a few things about us first or you won't believe what happened. First I'll write about me, and then Zelda can write about herself.

My full name is Henry Maximilian Ledniz. My parents gave me that name when I was born because they must have been odd even then. All the kids at school call me Henry and it's only when I come home to our apartment at 30 Lincoln Plaza that my berserk mother and father call me Henry Maximilian. Zelda lives a block away at 40 Lincoln Plaza with her parents, who are very different from mine, though she'll tell you about them when she feels like it. The main thing I need you to know now is that I'm very good-looking like Luke Skywalker, but in an alien sort of way. I'm just being truthful. People tell me how handsome I am. My mother kept me in a baby carriage for three extra years so I could be rolled in and out of Zabar's Delicatessen and the Nevada Meat Market to receive praise from other shoppers. Of course, I do have a few flaws. My first flaw is my hair. It is mouse brown with a cowlick that grows straight up out of my skull and needs a pound of mousse to subdue it. My hair is so thick that when I go to Pepe's Haircut Salon, where all the kids from my school go, Pepe has to use a thinning scissors like a hedge trimmer. He clips so much hair off my head that when it falls to the floor, it looks like a decapitated head. My eyes also pop out a little if you look closely, and there's a tiny scar to the right of my upper lip from when I was ten years old and ran through a glass door at the Magic Wok Cafe on Columbus Avenue. I should let you know that the middle-aged lady who works in Sedutto's ice cream parlor in the bottom of my building always flirts with me when I go in there for a fix of cookies 'n' cream. She says I'm going to be a real heartbreaker like Casanova when I grow up, but I'm fifteen already. Zelda, who is reading over my shoulder, just yelled at me for bragging about my looks, but I've got to be truthful. She says it'd be much better if I just told you things I *did* and then you'd know as much about me as you could stand.

Seven things I did last week are:

1) I bought a copy of the *Star Gazette* and read "Why Alex the beer-serving dog has become the surprising new star of TV's top 10 commercials."

2) I watched reruns of *Jaws I*, *Nightmare on Elm Street II*, and *Police Academy III.*

3) I went to the edge of Central Park to watch rats sunbathe on a rock.

4) I took Zelda to the Cosmic Soda Shoppe for a frozen hot chocolate and a macadamia nut cookie.

5) I had a dream I was flying inside a big, bright-red room that had a bamboo table with a candle burning on it. I think it was a sacrifice chamber.

6) I gave a dollar to a bum who was screaming for God and asking if God's real name was "Buddy."

7) I ordered fresh flowers for Miss Applebaum's grave.

Zelda says I shouldn't tell the following because it's irrelevant, but I often leave my calling card in phone booths. If you ever see the following, then you'll know Henry Ledniz was there:

Greetings
Homo Sapiens!
you, too, may become
EXTINCT!!!
Sincerely, Mr. Dino Saur

Zelda looks very cranky now, so I've got to let her get at the word processor.

Chapter Two

My name is Zelda Einnob and I *am* cranky about a lot of the things Henry wrote in the first chapter. There is simply no way I can make you understand what happened to us concerning Miss Applebaum's death unless you know more accurate things about us than Henry told you. He always thinks of the craziest way to do anything because he has a hard time facing up to anything that remotely resembles true emotion. *That* is Henry's main flaw, not his cowlick. Deep down, he is one of the most compassionate, loving boys in the world, but he'd be the last to show you. I have known him all my life and when I look back on our growing up together, I am filled with a great warmth and a strange, mystical belief that God really does exist. Without Henry, I don't think I could have survived all the frantic and nerve-wracking events that have happened.

Henry *is* very handsome. As he told you, everyone knows that, especially him. For myself, I always wanted to look like Elizabeth Taylor, Vivien Leigh, or Princess Di. I don't. I am just normal-looking except for my black hair, which reaches down to my shoulder blades. The reason I grew it that long was because I used to be in the children's chorus at the Metropolitan Opera, which is right across the street from my family's apartment. I'm not in the chorus now because I grew too big for the children's costumes, but the opera I loved being in the most was Puccini's *Turandot.* The head diva in that opera wears a long black wig in the second act, after a stranger correctly answers three riddles she asks him. The story of *Turandot* is that if this stranger doesn't know the answers to the riddles, he will have to face a distasteful fate. When I saw how beautiful and distinctive the diva looked, I immediately started letting my hair grow and I also started using a bit of English Lavender powder, crimson Max Factor lipstick, and Maybelline mascara. Henry doesn't need anything like makeup, but I need all the help I can get. I have taken a lot of singing and dancing lessons and I intend to go into a theatrical profession or be a psychiatrist. For a few examples of things I have done that would help you know me better, I am referring to my teachers' reports from last term because I feel they will present the most objective point of view.

1) WHAT MY ENGLISH TEACHER MRS. LARNER SAID ABOUT ME: "Zelda's assignments for English are always a pleasure to receive and brimming with insight. Her ballad on Marilyn Monroe's exploitation was a knockout."

2) LIBRARY SCIENCE WITH MR. WARWICK: "Zelda could refer to a dictionary with more regularity."

3) MATH WITH MISS GOLDBERG: "Miss Einnob worked well with the concept of 3-digit divisors and she performed well on hypotenuses."

4) FRENCH WITH MR. ALFIERI: "She effectively perceives the differences between living and dead languages."

5) HIGH SCHOOL CHORUS WITH MISS VROOMBA: "Zelda is now singing with a very wide range (almost three octaves in warm-ups), and is listening to others and trying to blend better with her soprano section. Her hair makes her a particularly impressive soloist."

6) ART WITH MR. LAHR: "Zelda's collage of a clay girl sitting in an aluminum tree works beautifully."

You also need to know a few ways that Henry and I are especially different. First of all, I have regular-size blue eyes and he has giant green eyes like a hawk. When we walk down the street, I look up at the buildings and treetops because I love how beautiful they are, but Henry checks the gutters for lost money. Also, he doesn't remember his dreams, but I remember mine and keep a record of them in a journal. Last night, I dreamed I was walking down Broadway and saw a mysterious girl with mushrooms growing out of her head. It was really very frightening. I remember trying to run away from her, but she chased me. When she got close, mushrooms started growing out of *my* head. I started pulling the mushrooms out of my skull, but the faster I did, the faster they grew! I woke up screaming, and when I told Henry about the dream, all he did was burp. Again, it was his way of avoiding emotion and not wanting to face up to anything connected to what happened to Miss Applebaum; I'm afraid that just won't do anymore.

It all started last September 9th around 8:30 in the morning. That was the first day after the summer vacation. Henry and I went in the 82nd Street entrance of Andrew Jackson along with about two thousand other noisy kids who were trying to get their programs and say hello to friends they hadn't seen all summer. Henry and I just went straight up to the third-floor science laboratory because we wanted to sign up immediately to be two of Miss Applebaum's lab assistants again, which is what we had been during the year before. We practically exploded through the door calling out, "Hi, Miss Applebaum!"

But there was no Miss Applebaum.

There was only a man we'd never seen before, in a white lab coat, and he looked slightly nervous.

"Miss Applebaum isn't here," he muttered, and continued setting up some kind of pulley system. "I'm her replacement," he added, "Mr. Greenfield."

"Is she giving up the lab?" Henry asked.

"No," Mr. Greenfield said, looking us over suspiciously.

"Then where is she?" I wanted to know.

"Miss Applebaum *retired.*"

There was something about the tone of this Mr. Greenfield's voice that was very neurotic, and the way he couldn't look us in the eye made me feel as if he knew some sort of secret. Some terrible secret.

I can't write any more at this moment. I'm sorry.

Chapter Three

Zelda is crying. She cries very easily because she's too sensitive for her own good. I have to tell you those things about her because she won't. She's too polite. Like when she told you about the young stranger in the opera. She said if he didn't know the answers to Turandot's riddles, he would have to face "a distasteful fate." She should have just told you that they would have chopped his head off. In fact, all through the opera, most of the stage is decorated with young men's heads that have been chopped off and stuck on bamboo sticks for Peking masses to behold.

Anyway, both Zelda and I felt very strange when this new lab teacher told us Miss Applebaum had retired. We weren't expecting it at all. Most kids might not feel whacked out about a teacher retiring, but Zelda and I think the loss of a devoted schoolteacher is an important event. We think a lot more of schoolteachers than they could ever imagine. We even like teachers we hate because we think of ways to drive them nuts. Teachers have always been powerful forces in Zelda's life and mine. When we were very little at elementary school, we thought teachers lived their whole lives inside of school buildings. We thought there were secret staircases that lowered down at night, and after the teachers got rid of the students for the day, they would go through mysterious passages to hidden condo units on the roof or to pup tents in the boiler room. I remember the time Zelda and I first saw a teacher outside of school. It was our principal, Miss McGillicuthey. She was walking down Fifth Avenue in the St. Patrick's Day parade, and we thought she had illegally escaped the school building.

But Miss Applebaum was the most special teacher we had ever met in our entire decade of academic pursuits. Her lab periods were in the morning, during which she was in charge of supplying all the equipment, chemicals, and paramecia that every science teacher would need. She was the only teacher who had the experience and training for such a vast job. After her lab preparations, she would teach only two classes. From the first day, Zelda and I had known we wanted to work with Miss Applebaum before school and during our free periods in order to be around her and all the fascinating gizmos in the science lab. Of course, we also earned extra service credits, but we would have helped clean test tubes and adjust Bunsen burners for nothing. There is no way I can tell you all the incredible things Miss Applebaum did to excite Zelda and me and all the kids in her classes. But the things she did when it was just her, Zelda, and me in the lab were spectacular. A few general highlights are:

a) Miss Applebaum once brought in over seventy cocoons from the park and hung them by threads from the windows. A month later, we came to class and there were seven million infant grasshoppers leaping all over the desks and causing a riot.

b) Another time, Miss Applebaum explained in scientific detail how doctors force a tapeworm out of a patient by giving massive doses of laxatives and then searching through buckets until they find the worm's head.

c) Last January, she let me demonstrate static electricity by permitting me to charge up Zelda on a Van de Graaff generator. A good time was had by all, except Zelda:

See? That's how provocative she was just in class, not to mention all the adventures she gave us searching for amoebas and using microscopes to spy on flies' legs and human cheek cells.

Zelda has stopped crying now and wants me to tell you a few things about the more artistic sides of Miss Applebaum. Well, I can't lie. She was extremely creative, but some of the things she did only explained why a certain faction of the faculty and kids thought she was eccentric. Basically, she baked bohemian ceramic earrings in the laboratory incubator during her spare time and sold them to other teachers who wanted bargain birthday, Xmas, and Chanukah gifts. Secondly, you might as well know that Miss Applebaum sometimes wore a black homburg hat on days when she wanted to feel "special." Also, it should be reported that Miss Applebaum represented the faculty in the school's spring amateur show by singing "Hello, Dolly" and "I'm Gonna Wash That Man Right outa My Hair." Unfortunately, she couldn't carry a tune very well, and some of the faculty and students thought she was beginning to act a little nuts.

I was the one who first suggested to Zelda that we visit Miss Applebaum and bring her a begonia plant from Ye Green Thumb Flower Shop as a token of how much we were going to miss her. Also, I think what really drove us to do it was we just couldn't believe she had really retired, and needed to hear it from the horse's mouth. As you probably know, a begonia is one of those plain little plants with small boring flowers on it that everyone gives as gifts because they can't afford to spend the money on a dozen roses anymore. The begonia we bought for Miss Applebaum only cost two dollars and ninety-eight cents, including the pot—but I knew it would be the kind of thing Miss Applebaum would make a big fuss over. She always loved anything living, even skunk cabbages.

We did know Miss Applebaum lived in the Saratoga Apartment House, which is a very humble building on Central Park West, but we didn't have her phone number. It was unlisted like everybody's in New York to avoid recorded solicitation calls from computerized big businesses. Besides, I thought it would be fun to surprise Miss Applebaum anyway, which turned out to be an extremely bad idea, but I didn't know it at the time. Anyway, on September ninth, Zelda and I agreed to purchase the begonia and bring it up to Miss Applebaum's immediately after school. We really loved her as a teacher, although we didn't know that much about her personal life. It's strange how you can actually grow to admire and adore teachers and not know very much about them. At school she had once in a while talked about the view she had of Central Park and that she lived on the eighth floor. And the only thing else we knew was some mornings when we worked for her she would talk about some of her neighbors in the building, but just in general, like if someone had gotten a new poodle or if an elderly person had broken a hip. Naturally, it does sound demented that two kids would think about bringing a plant to their retired science teacher on a Friday afternoon when most kids would be getting dressed for a trendy evening at Loew's Cineplex. Zelda says I've really got to tell about how strange my mother and father are, but I told her to hold her horses and that I'll get around to them soon enough. Actually, my mother is a psychoanalyst who I call the "Freudian Octopus" and my father is a math professor who I refer to as the "Cockaloony Bird." I'm not rude to them in their presence, of course. I'll tell you more about them later.

Anyway, Zelda and I got out of school at 3:05 on 82nd Street and we walked down Central Park West to Miss Applebaum's building, which is near the south corner of 67th Street. We had often walked by the building before and sometimes we'd remember that Miss Applebaum lived there, but it wasn't the kind of building that really caught your attention. It wasn't like the Dakota or the Parkington or any of the really fancy buildings that have people like Celeste Holm, Cher, or Yoko Ono and Sean living in them. The Saratoga really just always looked very insignificant with dull-brown bricks and underprivileged-looking gargoyles peering down from the top ledge. It had no doorman and a really worn brown canopy. Its one distinction was that it was just a stone's throw away from the building used at the end of *Ghostbusters* where the giant marshmallow monster gets zapped by laser guns and oozes white guck all over everybody.

When we got to Miss Applebaum's apartment house, we walked into the small outer lobby and Zelda held the begonia while I checked the apartment directory. There her name was: Alice Applebaum—8C.

"Maybe we should have written her first and told her we wanted to stop by," Zelda said.

"Then it wouldn't be a surprise," I pointed out, pressing the button for 8C.

"Well, maybe it shouldn't *be* a surprise."

We waited in the outer lobby expecting Miss Applebaum's crisp, happy voice to come over the intercom and ask who it was. Instead, only the release for the door sounded and we went right into the lobby, which desperately needed a paint job.

"She shouldn't buzz people straight in," Zelda said.

"Maybe her intercom isn't working," I suggested.

"I feel very funny about this."

"You feel funny about anything."

"I do not."

I pressed the button for the elevator, and its door opened. Zelda moaned and we got in. Then, I pressed the floor button and we started going up.

"Smells like ozone in here," I said, as the contraption started upward making clanking sounds.

"It does not," Zelda said, her eyes flitting nervously.

"Did you know an elevator fell last week in Paris?" I offered.

"No, I didn't."

"It had a nun and a chihuahua in it."

"Would you mind not telling me about it now?"

The elevator started to really creak and shake.

"The nun and chihuahua fell nine stories."

"Shut up, Henry."

"Don't you want to know if they got killed?"

"No, I don't."

"Well, they didn't. The nun was very quick thinking and, as the elevator fell, she suddenly picked the chihuahua up and jumped into the air."

Right this second, Zelda is getting a cranky look on her face like she's going to foam at the mouth if I don't let her get at the word processor, so I'd better before she pouts to death. I just wanted to tell you we got out of the elevator on the eighth floor and I thought we were in a haunted welfare hotel.

Chapter Four

The trouble with Henry is he doesn't really like any architecture or decorations that aren't hi-tech or filled with the shock of the new. The truth is that the hallway outside Miss Applebaum's apartment was very atmospheric and reminded me of the lovely old-fashioned wood trim found in the first act of *La Bohème* where the lead soprano knocks on the door and then faints. I've tried to teach Henry the sweetness of old things. I've pointed out the beauty of intricately carved moldings and how magical old wallpaper can be. To me, old wallpaper is like a mystical eye that has seen years and even decades of life walk by it. The wallpaper outside Miss Applebaum's apartment probably had molecules from people's breath and faint scents of perfumes and flavors of ancient coffeecakes, and probably the very essences of hundreds of humans who had passed by. Perhaps sweet and loving ghosts even lived in the wallpaper.

"What a joint," Henry said, ringing the buzzer outside apartment 8C.

"I still think we should have called," I repeated, turning the begonia in my hands so it could put its best flowers forward.

The door opened so fast, it startled me. A blast of sunlight coming from the windows made the form in front of us appear as a dark silhouette.

"What do you want?" the form asked. I recognized Miss Applebaum's voice, and the shape of her brown pixie-cut hair. But her voice was tired and weak.

"Hello, Miss Applebaum," I said.

"Hello," Henry said.

"It's Zelda Einnob and Henry Ledniz," I clarified.

Miss Applebaum shifted to the left and some of the hall light bounced off the door to reveal the delicate features of her face. She looked like a mature porcelain doll, dressed in a dark-blue terry-cloth bathrobe. Her face froze for a moment as she absorbed the sight of us, but then she broke into a tremendous smile of recognition.

"Oh, my goodness," she laughed with much more energy. "Come in! Come in!"

"I know we should have called you, but we didn't have your phone number," I apologized.

Henry moved quickly inside like the nosy boy he is. I went in and politely concentrated on Miss Applebaum as I presented her with the begonia.

"What beautiful little stars!" she exclaimed, lifting up the tiny pink flowers to get a closer look at them. "Oh my, oh my," she added as she closed the door.

"We don't want to bother you," I said. Henry was already drifting toward the living room and seemed to be sizing up everything in sight.

"I was expecting my doctor from Weehawken," Miss Applebaum apologized, tightening the cloth belt of her robe.

"We can leave," I offered.

"Oh, no."

"Maybe another time would be better?" I asked.

"Of course not," she insisted. "It's wonderful to see you. Wonderful!"

She led the way through the foyer and into a very large living room beyond. I was so nervous, I didn't dare to look around at first. I just kept my attention on Miss Applebaum, but I knew I wasn't in any normal living room. I was catching glimpses of strange massive things out of the corner of my eye and I was very aware of Henry flitting here and there with uncontrollable excitement.

"I have to sit down," Miss Applebaum said, panting. "Please sit."

"Of course," I said.

She sat down slowly onto an antique blue-and-white wicker sofa and I sat next to her. I could see how she wasn't the usual sparkling Miss Applebaum we had known from school. I mean, she had the same kind face, but she looked very tired. This was the first time Henry or I had ever seen a teacher in a bathrobe. Actually, Miss Applebaum looked rather charming and elegant, but she was still breathing strangely. I thought maybe she had been doing exercises or perhaps had climbed a ladder to change a lightbulb, but then I realized her breathing probably had something to do with the doctor she was expecting.

"Do you have a cold?" Henry asked straight out. I wanted to kick him. What was worse, he said it to Miss Applebaum but was looking at me and blinking his huge hawk eyes frantically in some sort of crazed signal. I knew he wanted me to turn around and look at the rest of the room, but I didn't dare yet.

"It's just a slight cold," Miss Applebaum wheezed.

At that second, the buzzer sounded.

"Excuse me," Miss Applebaum said, getting up and pressing the lobby door release. "This must be Dr. Obitcheck now."

"We really should go," I whispered to Henry.

"We really should *stay*," he said firmly, his eyes still flying all over the place.

I don't know what was wrong with me, but I still couldn't look around the room. All I could see was Miss Applebaum moving slowly toward the front door still holding the begonia. I was mesmerized until the elevator clanged its way to the outer hallway. The apartment buzzer sounded and Miss Applebaum opened the door. The man she let in was around fifty, tall with gray hair, and he wore a dark, wrinkled, pin-striped suit. Miss Applebaum and he exchanged a few words of greeting, and then she led him to the edge of the living room.

"These are two of my former students," Miss Applebaum said proudly.

Henry and I nodded and smiled, and it was then I noticed Dr. Obitcheck had the most unusual pair of eyes I'd ever seen in my life. His left one looked normal. It seemed to be peering at me in an alert professional manner. But his right eye was mainly all white except for a little blue circle that was frozen in the far right staring at the floor. The result was really frightening because I couldn't tell which eye was really looking at me. I didn't know which part of his face to relate to.

"How nice of you to stop by," Dr. Obitcheck said, his eyes shifting into ever stranger positions as he clutched a Jack the Ripper type of black satchel.

"Thank you," Henry said, and I could tell by the sound of his voice he too was mesmerized by the doctor's eyeballs.

"Dr. Obitcheck has to give me a brief treatment," Miss Applebaum explained, setting the begonia down on a side table. "Please just make yourselves at home." She smiled, muffled a cough, and disappeared with the doctor down a hallway. They weren't out of sight for a second before Henry was yanking my sleeve and repeating, "Look! Look! Look!"

Now and only now could I let myself turn and focus on the complete living room. I was shocked! I had glimpsed clutter, but what was in that room took my breath away. The area looked like a dense jungle, a startling laboratory, a library, and a storage room all rolled into one. I have always loved plants, so I'd better describe those first. There were ficus trees, hanging baskets of ivy, pots of split-leaf philodendrons, dried cat-o'-nine-tails, anthuriums, a dozen or so other large plants I didn't know the names of, geraniums, marigolds, snapdragons, snake plants, cacti, orchids, lilies, and the only indoor huge lilac bush I'd ever seen in my life. The plants completely dominated a vast window area and reached to the top of the extra-high ceiling. The late-afternoon sunlight bounced into the room, but most of the light came from a large cluster of fluorescent lightbulbs just above one of the most unusual flower-growing machines I had ever seen. Long trays of small potted plants sat on a Ferris wheel device, which rotated very slowly, lifting rows and rows of gloxinias, African violets, spider plants, lilies of the valley, and herbs upward toward the light and then down again. I saw at least thirty begonias that were twice as big as the one we had brought. There were plants in every nook and cranny.

Then the second shock concerning the contents of the room hit me. The clutter that was piled up over ten feet high on both sides of the living room began to have a rhyme and reason to it. It consisted of the strangest pieces of scientific equipment I had ever seen, except for one or two pieces I recognized from the laboratory storeroom at school. There was a huge model of an ear and a giant model of an atom that had been in the school lab when Henry and I had started working for Miss Applebaum, but they had been replaced by updated models last term. I had never thought about what happened to outmoded science equipment from our school, but I knew I had found out. The entire living room was filled with what amounted to scientific antiques. There was a wind tunnel to demonstrate airplane flight using model rudders and ailerons. There were eight old barometers, scientific jars, and Petri dishes. There was a life-size pull-apart demonstration model of the human digestion system. Seven beautiful black-and-gold-trimmed microscopes. A set-up of the sun and planets to show phases of the moon and perform eclipses. There were test-tube racks and open boxes of one-, two-, and three-hole rubber stoppers. Tripods. An empty 80-gallon aquarium. There was a 3-foot model of a flower blossom with its stamen and pistil and petals showing. Against the wall behind the sofa was a stand with a real human skeleton hanging from it. I recognized it from school because it had a few missing ribs and a cracked skull from when one of the lab workers had accidentally knocked it over and a newer skeleton had been ordered. There was a very large stainless steel coffee table in the center of the room with the bones of a frog and an old stuffed alligator. There were corroding batteries on shelves and a collection of giant magnets with sprinklers of iron fillings. There were gears and telegraph keys and static electricity rods and a radio receiver and earphones and chemicals and a ladder leaning against the highest pile of equipment. Henry was touching everything. He did nothing but let out squeals of delight as he found still bigger magnets. And he discovered a break in the vegetation! We could see then that the living room was actually L-shaped. Henry moved vines aside and started on around the bend.

"*Don't,*" I ordered.

"Why not?"

"We should wait for Miss Applebaum."

"She said to make ourselves at home."

Henry's eyes now moved like radar cones, searching deeper and deeper into the greenery and stacks of equipment. I followed him around the bend of the living room.

Suddenly, he halted.

"What's the matter?" I asked.

Henry didn't say a word. He stopped breathing. I moved closer to him, whispering to him, saying, "I think we should go back to the wicker furniture and just sit down and wait." I told him I was feeling a little scared. I was really on the verge of an anxiety attack.

And then I saw the look in his eyes. I could see even he was frightened now. I moved next to him, trying to see what he was seeing.

Then I did.

There, beyond a cluster of potted plants, past the leaves of a giant fern, was another door at the very end of the living room. It was like being in a maze, because from that doorway we could see across a small, shadowy kitchen and in through still another door to a back bedroom. Miss Applebaum was sitting on the edge of a bed, her back to us. She had draped her bathrobe off her shoulders and the white skin of her back could be seen in the light from a lamp. She appeared helpless, a delicate old doll, as Dr. Obitcheck moved a chair next to her and began to press a very large needle into her skin.

Chapter Five

When Zelda says a needle is very large, that means it was really very, *very* large. She caught only a glimpse of it and disappeared back into the living room so fast it wasn't funny. That left me peeking through the ubiquitous leaves to see the whole thing. What it was was a humongous hypodermic needle. The needle was at least six inches long, and the chamber that's supposed to hold the medicine was a cylinder about three inches wide and eight inches long. The strangest thing about it all was I could see Dr. Obitcheck put the needle into Miss Applebaum's side, but he wasn't pushing the handle on the hypodermic to put any medicine *in*, he was taking some kind of fluid *out* of Miss Applebaum until it filled the cylinder. It was like a reverse injection, and to tell you the truth, that was all I wanted to see, so I tiptoed back into the front part of the living room and sat on a wicker footstool across from Zelda.

"We have to get out of here," Zelda said in a desperate whisper.

"We can't just disappear!"

"What is he *doing* to her?"

For once, I didn't have an answer. We both just sat still surrounded by the vines and leaves and the labyrinth of scientific apparati. Our ears strained to listen. We were shocked to hear, suddenly, Miss Applebaum laughing. Then there came footsteps and chatting as Miss Applebaum and Dr. Obitcheck came back down the hall and appeared again. Both of them seemed better for the experience, although Dr. Obitcheck's eyes each shot off in different directions like cat's-eye marbles. He was making small talk again, but we couldn't tell exactly who he was making small talk with. He carried his black leather satchel, which I knew had his equipment in it. He said good-bye to us, his eyes did a last flip-flop, and then he went out the door. With him gone, Miss Applebaum came toward us with a great smile on her face, and she began speaking like the bundle of energy we had always known her as at school. Now she wasn't wheezing or breathing strangely at all.

"We'd better be going now," Zelda said.

"Oh, no, please stay," Miss Applebaum pleaded. In a flash she picked up the begonia we had brought her and carried it to the plant Ferris wheel at the window. "Here you go round the mulberry bush!" she started to sing as she put the plant on a lower slat, gave it a shot of mist from a spray gun, and fast forwarded the wheel until the plant was high into the uppermost sunlight. "Oh, it's a beautiful new soul," she said, "a beautiful new soul."

I looked at Zelda and she looked at me. I could tell we both were thinking Miss Applebaum wasn't mentally exactly like when we knew her in school. She was colorfully odd then, but it was clear there had to be something drastically wrong with her or a doctor with weird eyes wouldn't have to come and stick her with a syringe the size of a basketball pump. But when she turned from the Ferris wheel and looked at us, all I could see was sadness.

"I'll cherish your gift," she said.

"We're so glad you like it," I said. I really was.

"Yes," Zelda added.

"We missed you at school."

"We really did."

"I miss school so much," Miss Applebaum said, and her eyes had a faraway look in them. For a moment, it seemed her mind had flown off into memory, but she quickly snapped out of it.

"Can I get you some yogurt?" she asked.

"No, thank you," Zelda said too quickly.

"Please stay and have yogurt."

"We really can't."

"I have mixed fruit, lemon, and boysenberry."

"Boysenberry," I requested.

"We can't."

"Which flavor would you like?" Miss Applebaum pressed Zelda. "Lemon?"

"No, thank you."

"I'm out of raspberry."

"We really have to be going."

"Please have lemon. You'll love the lemon."

Now I gave Zelda a dirty look. "She'll have the lemon."

"Good!" Miss Applebaum exclaimed. "One boysenberry, one lemon, and I'll have a mixed fruit!"

In a flash she was gone for the kitchen, and Zelda leaned forward practically hissing at me.

"I hate yogurt," Zelda said.

"Everyone does."

"I want to leave."

"I thought you liked Miss Applebaum."

"I do."

"Then be nice to her."

"There's something wrong."

"What gave you the clue?" I asked, moving a leafy philodendron stalk off my shoulder.

In a flash, Miss Applebaum was back with individual Dannon yogurts and spoons.

"There. We'll pretend we're having a little picnic," she said, sitting on the floor with her back to the model of the human digestion system.

"I am so glad you stopped by. All morning, I kept remembering a puzzle and I wanted someone to try it out on."

"What puzzle?" I asked.

"The one about nine dots."

"Nine dots?"

Zelda gave me a "shut up" look.

"Yes," she said, moving right onto the floor with a pencil and sheet of paper. "Nine dots like *this.*" She demonstrated:

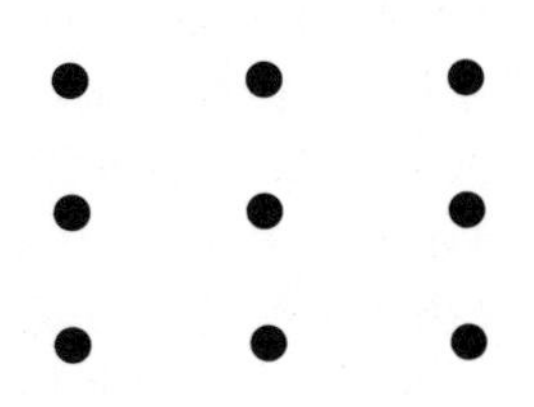

"Do you know this puzzle?" she wanted to know, her eyes starting to really glow.

"No, we don't," Zelda and I admitted.

"Oh, it's a wonderful puzzle," Miss Applebaum exclaimed. "What you have to do is connect *all* the dots with four straight lines, without lifting your pencil off the paper."

"That's easy," I said.

"Oh, please do it, then." Miss Applebaum clapped her hands in joy.

"Sure," I said, taking the pencil. I mean, it looked so simple, I figured an idiot could do it. I just quickly did straight lines through all of the dots like this:

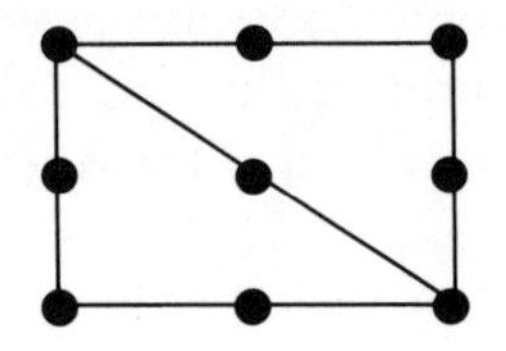

"There," I said.

"Oh, no," Miss Applebaum laughed. "You used *five* lines, not *four*."

"Let me try it," Zelda said. And then she tried it and she failed, and then I tried it another way and I failed, and Miss Applebaum had to get us a lot more paper and we tried dozens and dozens of times, but neither Zelda nor I could get four straight lines to connect all the dots. Miss Applebaum just laughed and laughed. After my forty-third attempt, Miss Applebaum sensed I was ready to scream. She simply said, "Here, let me show you the answer."

"I want to figure it out myself."

"No, you don't," Zelda said.

"Yes, I do."

"No."

"Yes."

"Oh, this is such fun," Miss Applebaum giggled, and precisely at that moment it seemed as though the three of us were back in school having fun in the lab like we always had. It was as though nothing had changed.

But it had.

"I would like to know the answer," I said softly.

Miss Applebaum drew a new set of dots, and her eyes filled with delight as she used only four straight lines to connect all the dots.

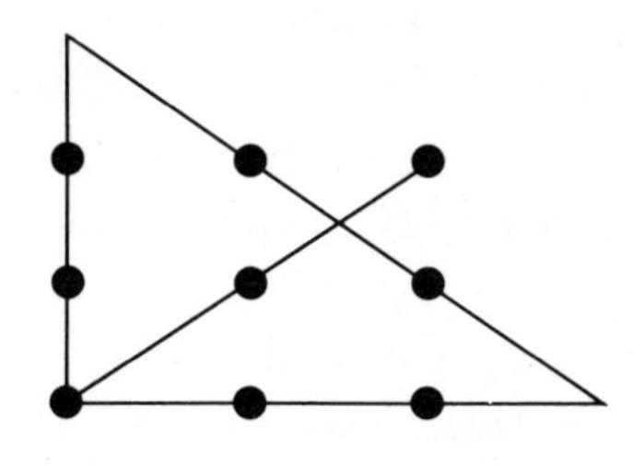

"You see, the answer lies in going beyond what you would expect." She smiled. "The secret of the nine dots is like the secret of life itself. The true answers are always beyond our expectations. We just have to use our imaginations!"

"Well, we really have to be going now," Zelda said.

"Yes, we do."

"But won't you come back tomorrow?"

"I don't think we can."

"Please," Miss Applebaum pleaded.

"Perhaps another day," Zelda said. "We'll call next time."

When Miss Applebaum saw us stand up and start edging for the door, she looked frightened and ran for a piece of paper. "Here's my phone number. I'll be waiting. Maybe you can at least call and talk to me. . . ."

"Yes, of course," Zelda said, taking the phone number and putting it in her pocket.

"We can always call," I murmured.

"There are so many things we can do now that I'm retired," Miss Applebaum blurted, her eyes growing suddenly shiny. She moved about like a desperate waltzing mouse as I opened the door. She poured out desperately now, as though she only had seconds before being sent before a firing squad.

"We'll play Elevator Roulette, and Goonie. We'll go to Central Park! Do you ever go to Central Park?" she asked.

"We don't like Central Park," I said.

"We went there when we were kids," Zelda added.

"Why don't you like the park?" Miss Applebaum asked me.

"Too many bums and muggings," I said.

"Oh, no," Miss Applebaum corrected. "You've got to let me show you the park. There are games we can play. Wonderful things I can show you. Secrets. I'll take you for a ride on the Central Park roller coaster. . . ."

"There is no roller coaster in Central Park," I pointed out.

"Oh, there is! There is! You just haven't seen it!" Miss Applebaum cried out.

"Good-bye, Miss Applebaum," Zelda said, practically running to the elevator and pressing the call button.

"Yes, we'll see you," I said, heading down the hall. In a moment the elevator had arrived and we stepped inside. Miss Applebaum stood in the doorway of her apartment, clutching her bathrobe with one hand and waving frantically.

She called, "Thank you for the begonia! Thank you! Oh god, thank you. We'll have such wonderful times in the park!"

The elevator door closed and we were gone.

Chapter Six

After we left Miss Applebaum's apartment, Henry insisted we go to the Cosmic Soda Shoppe for our usual frozen hot chocolate. My head was spinning from the images of leaves and wicker and strange eyes and microscopes, but Henry just kept talking on and on about what a unique experience we had just had.

We sat in our usual booth, which is one on the side wall with a view of the street, because Henry likes to keep an eye out in case any cars go out of control and crash through the window. That kind of thing happens in Manhattan more than most people think. We always hear the screeching of brakes and see at least one extraordinary accident per week. Within the last three months alone we saw a pin-striped Dodge van crash into the Ballet Expresso Luncheonette, and a Tourarama bus jumped the curve and demolished Marie's Deep Pan Pizza. Broadway is a truly dangerous vehicular area and you have to be very alert.

"Two frozen hot chocolates," Henry ordered for us from Large Marge, our favorite waitress. She's always very nice to us and gives us milkshake dividends and the biggest scoops of ice cream.

The Cosmic Soda Shoppe has a secret formula that Henry and I could never exactly figure out, but we think they take ice cubes with a cup of very thick hot chocolate and do something with it in a blender. Then they pour it into fancy frappe dishes and top the whole thing off with a five-inch layer of whipped cream. It's very delicious and emotionally comforting, especially if you've just been through a terrifying ordeal.

"Wasn't she fascinating?" Henry blurted.

"Who?"

"Who do you think?"

"Miss Applebaum?"

"Yes."

"Are you crazy?"

"She's so *different* than at school."

"Of course, she's different. There's something very wrong with her," I stressed.

"Not really," Henry insisted. "Maybe when she was teaching, we just never really saw this side of her."

I refused to even look at Henry for five minutes while he babbled on about how maybe Miss Applebaum had acted a little more eccentric than usual, but that basically she was still the same person we knew at Andrew Jackson High. Henry has a special way of fast-talking when he thinks he's going to steamroll something past me, trick me into doing something I wouldn't do willingly in a million years. Actually, I suppose that's another one of the differences between Henry and me. He's always instigating uncommon behavior, getting us involved in action when I'd prefer to avoid it. I'm much more interested in what everything *means*, but Henry doesn't care to analyze very much at all.

"She's ill." I finally was able to get a word in edgewise.

"She probably just had a little cold," Henry observed.

"Are you out of your mind?!"

"You're going to make a big thing out of the doctor, aren't you?"

"A big thing?" I practically screamed. "You saw the size of that hypodermic! Even her mind's different!"

"Are you saying she's nuts?"

"I didn't say that."

"Yes, you did."

"Henry, there's something terribly wrong with Miss Applebaum."

"You look scared stiff."

"I am not."

The frozen hot chocolates arrived, and Large Marge had put a special cherry on the top. I couldn't get my straw into mine soon enough and was hoping Henry would shut up and sip, but he didn't.

"Maybe this is how people get when they retire," Henry offered, but I could see he didn't believe that one for a minute.

"It was wrong for us to go there."

"She loved the begonia! She loved it!" Henry said. "Doesn't it make you want to bring her another?"

"No, it does not. She's got dozens of begonias!"

"I think she really wants to see us again."

"No, she doesn't."

"Aren't you being selfish?" Henry accused.

I absolutely refused to answer.

"Aren't you the least bit interested in learning how to play Elevator Roulette, or Goonie, or going for a ride on the Central Park roller coaster?"

"No, I'm not! There *is* no roller coaster in Central Park and you know that!"

"Don't you even *care* about her? She taught us so much. She made us love science. She let us hide out in the lab whenever we wanted. She gave us excessive service credits. She was our teacher, Zelda," he reminded me. "Our *teacher.* And she *wanted* us to stay!"

"I know," I said.

"Doesn't that count for anything?" he pleaded, opening wide his huge eyes.

I didn't get home that night until after six o'clock and my mother was cooking dinner. "Where were you?" she asked.

"With Henry," I said.

"That's nice." My mother was beginning to bread pork chops and pop them into a frying pan. "I got your father free tickets to a Rangers hockey game, so he went with Uncle Joe. Please drain the string beans, honey," she added.

You might as well know now that my mother works in a high school as a schoolteacher, too. Specifically, she's a guidance counselor. In fact, a lot of the West Side of New York is filled with teachers, and I suppose that's because there are so many kids, schools, and rent-controlled apartments. My mom is at Jefferson High on 112th Street, where kids are much rougher than at my school, and she always comes home with a tale of some new behavioral problem—like how a kid spray-painted the principal or threw eggs at the Latin teacher. And my father's a librarian for a chemical research library downtown, so neither of my parents makes very much money by New York standards. What they are very rich in, however, is love. They are two of the most caring and dedicated people I have ever known. My mother is short and has a sweet face like a beloved character actress with a perm, and my father looks a little like Stan Laurel, the silent-movie star. They both are wonderfully kind. My mother talks a lot. If you didn't know her, you'd think she was a big gossip. She's not. She's just insecure and thinks if she knows everything going on in New York, people won't look down on her. She's always been overweight and I know she doesn't think she's very pretty, although she tries very hard. My father is a very quiet, gentle man who is immediately likeable, and sometimes I catch my mother staring at him during dinner. I think she wonders what he could have ever seen in her. She doesn't realize my father has always adored and worshiped her personality and good heart. In his eyes she is very beautiful. She brings him up to date on *The New York Times* best-sellers or takes him to see a Broadway drama on student discount tickets. He kisses her and compliments her on being *au courant*, and at least once a week he thanks her in front of me for giving him a great daughter. Of course that always makes me feel wonderful.

Charming.

That's what my parents are.

Sincere and *charming.*

I finished with the string beans and started to set the table as my mother began cutting up a salad.

"How is Henry?" she asked.

"Fine."

I knew it wouldn't take long before she'd know practically everything I did that day. She asks me a lot of questions, but I don't mind because she is really interested. More than anything, I feel she desperately wants to share my growing up with me.

"We brought a begonia over to Miss Applebaum," I said casually.

There was a bit of a pause as my mother diced a carrot.

"That was very nice of you."

I detected a strange tone in her voice. "Is something wrong?"

"No."

"Are you sure, Mom?"

"I just heard that she was ill," she said.

"How did you know?"

"The nurse at my school knows the nurse at your school," my mother said, sounding rather guarded, I thought. I forgot how networked my mom is through most of the schools on the West Side. A lot of the teachers at her school are friends with teachers at my school. On top of that, my mom "schmoozes," as she calls it, with all of my teachers during PTA meetings and neighborhood apartment alliance meetings and events like that.

"Is something wrong, Mom?" I asked.
"No," she said.
"Yes, there is."
"No, there isn't."
"It's about Miss Applebaum, isn't it?"
"No, not really."
"*Please* tell me." I could see a sadness creep into her eyes.
"Oh, honey, I'm sorry. . . ."
"You *did* hear something, didn't you, Mom?"
"I shouldn't tell you. I know how much Miss Applebaum meant to you all last year. . . ."
"What? What's wrong?" I pleaded.
My mother has almost never lied to me. She often protects me from the truth about certain things or waits until she thinks I'm old enough to understand. She put her arms around me and gave me a hug.
"I heard Miss Applebaum's *very* ill," she finally said, sadly. "I'm sorry, honey. I'm very sorry, but that's what I heard. . . ."
I burst into tears because I knew what she meant. And I knew it was true. My mom just let me cry in her arms as I told her about the horrible hypodermic needle and the doctor at Miss Applebaum's. My mom told me everything she had heard from Miss Winters, the nurse at our high school, and she had even been told more details by someone who knew Mr. Kennedy, the assistant principal, who had helped file Miss Applebaum's medical retirement forms. Miss Applebaum had retired because she was terminally ill with cancer.

"But they can treat cancer now," I said.

"It must be too late for Miss Applebaum," my mom said softly.

"How can it be?"

"Sometimes it is," my mom said.

Later that night, Henry called me. I hadn't called him because I wanted to be alone and just try to sort things out in my mind. Henry knows whenever anything goes terribly wrong in my life and I'm completely overwhelmed. He senses it through the air like ESP and calls or rings the doorbell. All I remember is telling him about Miss Applebaum, and for the first time, he didn't have a snappy answer or a crazy idea to fix everything.

"Now we've *got* to go see her again."

The next day was Saturday and Henry met me in the lobby of my building at 9:30 A.M. He did look very tall and handsome, dressed in faded jeans and a sweatshirt that said: "KEEP AMERICA BEAUTIFUL: SWALLOW YOUR BEER CANS!" He had already called Miss Applebaum and told me she was thrilled that we wanted to go to the park with her. He said she sounded perfectly fine on the phone and didn't breathe strangely at all. In fact, when he had offered to stop by for her, she said she'd meet us at the 72nd Street park entrance because she had a little shopping to do first.

"She didn't sound like she was dying at all," Henry said, although we both knew that people with cancer, even the most deadly kinds, usually don't show symptoms in the early stages.

We walked to the corner of 64th and Central Park West. From there, it was only eight blocks north to where we were supposed to meet Miss Applebaum.

"What they're saying about her illness could be just a mistake," I said.

"Of course," Henry agreed, flipping a shock of hair out of his eyes.

"Somebody could have mixed up medical records or glanced at the wrong chart."

"Doctors make all kinds of mistakes, particularly when they have eyes like Dr. Obitcheck's and come from Weehawken," Henry agreed. "A man in my building knew someone who had a triple bypass and an X ray showed the surgeon had left a rubber glove in when he sewed him up."

As we walked uptown, several blind people came tapping toward us with white canes because there's a school for the blind on 67th Street. On our right were a lot of benches lining the long stone wall that marks the west boundary on Central Park; a number of derelicts and homeless people were still sleeping on them. A few were awake and staring at Henry's sweatshirt and my long black hair as though *we* were the peculiar ones. If I ever do become a psychologist, I would like to do a study on homeless people and what can be done to help them. It's awful how they have to live!

At some points, the park lawns rose high enough beyond the wall so we could see other poor people who had built little shelters out of cardboard and rags amidst the rocks and bushes. And just to the right of the sidewalk were gratings covering deep subway air shafts. Every few minutes, the ground would shake as a train rumbled by below, and stale air from the underground labyrinth would blow up like a Minotaur on the loose. Taxis, buses, trucks, and cars were already honking and bustling up and down the street. Kitchen workers sat playing poker outside the service entrance of Tavern on the Green restaurant. At one point I noticed for the first time a building on the left side of the street with dark archways that looked like the entrance to a mausoleum. I knew I was projecting all the fear I had inside of me over Miss Applebaum. As Henry and I approached 72nd Street, we could see the famous Dakota apartment house where many rich celebrities live. Every time Henry and I walk by it, we both grow very silent for a number of reasons. Usually, one of us mentions the movie filmed there where Mia Farrow gives birth to Satan's baby. And most of all, we can never forget that John Lennon was murdered in front of the huge black gates. My mother told me Yoko Ono still lives there and owns five apartments, and there is a rumor that one of the persons who tried to save John Lennon's life often goes to parties and brags that he kept John Lennon's bloodstained tie. I think that person must have a very deep-rooted psychological problem of his own.

There was no sign of Miss Applebaum as we crossed to the park. A tree with an enormous trunk reached its branches upward to the sky. Several of its limbs had been cut off or shaved off by lightning, and although it was still only September, there was a crisp, cool smell of autumn in the air. Henry and I decided to wait by a sign that proclaimed the rules of the park:

1) NO LOUD NOISES OR DEFACING OF PARK PROPERTY.

2) FAILURE TO LEASH A DOG IS A PUNISHABLE OFFENSE. FINE $50.

3) JOGGERS MUST USE DESIGNATED LANES.

4) NO ALCOHOL, DRUGS, OR ROCKET LAUNCHINGS.

After we read the sign, we noticed a bag lady sleeping on a bench near a hot-dog peddler. My heart practically broke just to look at her. She had ripped stockings and one leg hanging over the top rung of the bench, and half of her body was covered with newspapers. Three squirrels were looking at her as if they knew something was very wrong.

"There she is!" Henry blurted.

I turned to see Miss Applebaum wearing her black homburg hat and marching toward us from across the street. She was already waving and smiling, and I was surprised to see her dressed in a familiar earth-colored suit and carrying the same big leather briefcase she used to lug to school. It wasn't that she had a lot of clothes, but I had always noticed the things she *did* have were made of sturdy wool of tasteful colors.

"Hi," she said, beaming, and she lifted her hat for a moment and brushed a hand through the bangs of her pixie hair. "I hope I haven't kept you waiting?"

"Oh, no," Henry said.

"Not at all," I said, thinking how much she looked

like she was just arriving to punch the school time clock and go to work.

"I see you've already found *Helen*." Miss Applebaum smiled.

"Helen?" I inquired.

Miss Applebaum took a white bakery bag out of her briefcase and placed it on the bench near the sleeping bag lady.

"Breakfast time, Helen! Here's your bagel!" Miss Applebaum practically sang. The bag lady, without opening her eyes, reached over her head and grabbed the white bag. Then she clutched it to her body, straightened her newspapers, and went back to sleep.

"Come, come, come," Miss Applebaum said to us, and set off into the park at a good clip. "I have so many things to show you!"

Henry and I scooted after her into the first area of the park, which had a sign announcing "Strawberry Fields" because Yoko Ono had donated the money to make it a memorial to John Lennon. We walked over a tiled circle that had the word "IMAGINE" on it; on a nearby lawn was a group of people sitting cross-legged in a circle, chanting and doing yoga exercises.

"I just love the park!" Miss Applebaum bubbled, still keeping a good pace. "It's so alive! So alive!" Miss Applebaum didn't sound like she was dying at all.

Actually, Henry and I hadn't come to this part of the park in a long time. When we were very young, our parents would bring us to the park playgrounds and sandboxes and the Children's Zoo and places like that, but we never thought about it these days. The only thing we'd heard about the park for years now was that it was a dangerous place with things like diplomats getting mugged and all sorts of awful events.

"*That* tree is just beautiful in the spring," Miss Applebaum said, waving at a magnolia.

"I'll bet," Henry said.

"Isn't it a gorgeous day? Gorgeous! Gorgeous! Gorgeous!" Miss Applebaum's eyes sparkled.

"Yes," I agreed, thankful to see how well she was still breathing. Just looking at her happy face made me question the rumor my mother had heard.

Pigeons moved out of our way. A horse and carriage drove by in the distance. There were beautiful exotic bushes and white birch trees. Actually, Strawberry Fields was landscaped like no other part of the park. Mimosa trees. Shaped hedges. Berry bushes. A bag couple stretched out sunning themselves on a rock slab.

"I want to show you Genius's Walk, and my favorite statues, and, of course, we'll go for a ride on the Central Park roller coaster," she twinkled.

Henry looked ready to blurt out again that there was no roller coaster in Central Park, but I shot him a dirty look and he shut his mouth for a change. He just kept saying, "Coo, coo, coo," to the pigeons.

Miss Applebaum led us along the main path of asphalt lined with cobblestones, as joggers passed us. They each had their own style of clothes and motion. Then we came out of Strawberry Fields and crossed a roadway with dozens of bicyclists wearing all sorts of costumes. One man was riding in a purple suit and wearing a panama hat. A woman rode by dressed all in yellow. Then there was a boy with a live parrot on his shoulder. Deeper into the park, we passed the first statue.

"Do you know Daniel Webster?" Miss Applebaum asked, indicating the statue.

"No, not really," I said.

"Oh, he was a remarkable American statesman and a great orator. Great! Good morning, Mr. Webster," Miss Applebaum said, still keeping up a good pace. "Oh, Henry and Zelda, I have so much left to teach you! So much!"

Farther on, there were little briar patches and fir trees and a very big rock with a statue of a boy letting loose a magnificent bird.

"That's the Falconer," Miss Applebaum said, smiling. "Isn't he beautiful?"

It *was* very dramatic, I thought, and wondered why Henry and I had never noticed that statue before. In fact, the farther we got into the park and began to see it through Miss Applebaum's eyes, the more we realized how much of the park we had never really known. Of course, we did know for certain there was no roller coaster, and I dreaded the thought that Miss Applebaum might actually try to show us one.

Across from the Falconer was a side road that curved around in a circle, and we saw a long van and a group of people filming a commercial. That is a sight we often see all over the city. They're always filming some model in front of a trendy Japanese restaurant or closing a street so they can do a car chase for a TV show. Henry and I used to stop and ask what they were doing, but now we barely noticed them anymore. Even Miss Applebaum didn't mention them.

"Oh, they're playing bocci!" Miss Applebaum exclaimed as we walked by a field of old men and women dressed in very cute white sport outfits and rolling steel balls. "They play every weekend," Miss Applebaum said.

Soon we walked by Park Department vehicles, a mob of rollerskaters blasting portable stereos, and a boy with a guitar. Then came a concession stand called the Mineral Springs Health Bar.

"Would you like a Fudgsicle?" Miss Applebaum asked.

"Oh, no," I said.

"I would," Henry said.

"Wonderful," Miss Applebaum laughed, and she ordered one Fudgsicle and *fourteen* hot dogs.

"Hold this, please," Miss Applebaum asked, giving me her briefcase. She paid for everything, gave Henry his ice cream, and had all the hot dogs put on a cardboard tray.

"Excuse me a moment," Miss Applebaum said, dashing to a row of benches where she started passing out the hot dogs to a group of homeless people lying there. She also gave them some money, calling over her shoulder, "Have some nice hot coffee now!" After she gave everything away, she came bounding back to us, taking her briefcase. She marched us onward.

"So much to do, so much to do!" Miss Applebaum

declared. We passed a field with a sign that said "THIS AREA RESERVED FOR QUIET RECREATION," and there were a lot of people flying kites, picnicking, and throwing Frisbees.

"Isn't it beautiful?!" Miss Applebaum cried, as we zipped by mothers pushing baby carriages and children hopping on pogo sticks. One lady was pushing twins in a double stroller, and before the mother could stop her, Miss Applebaum bought them each a helium balloon. I felt very concerned about Miss Applebaum spending so much money, but I was glad to see how energetic she was. Psychologists might say I was experiencing an "approach-avoidance" situation, and maybe I should have said something, but I didn't. Henry, on the other hand, was having a great time. There were all sorts of people all over the park. An Oriental woman was brushing a white poodle. Young boys and girls were playing hopscotch. People were talking Spanish, French, and German. There was a police patrol in a blue truck. A statue of two eagles feasting on a dead goat with a date written as MDCCCLXIII. Then came a bust of Victor Herbert and people with all sorts of balloons including silver ones shaped like crescents and stars. At one clearing we could see in the distance the skyline of all the towering apartments that lined the park and marked its separation from the rest of the city. Streetlights made of black metal and curved to hold translucent globes lined the paths. Then we headed into a grove of very old giant trees, their branches shutting out most of the sun. A few leaves had begun to fall already and they spun around our feet like wisps of gold. There were huge maples. Oaks. Sycamores. A girl walked by with her hair shaved except for a pigtail on the back of her head. I no sooner heard the sound of a calliope than Miss Applebaum exclaimed, "Oh, *do* let's ride the carousel!" She rushed down a small hill and across a field. Within minutes, Miss Applebaum had us on the Central Park carousel, which is very famous and very real.

"Is this what you meant by the roller coaster?" Henry asked.

"Oh, heavens, no," Miss Applebaum said, sitting atop a white-and-silver wooden horse that went up and down as the carousel spun. "The roller coaster is entirely different." Miss Applebaum laughed, and then grabbed the reins as though she were riding a horse at Belmont. Her homburg hat flipped up and down as we went around.

Riding the carousel brought back memories of my mother taking me to the carousel when I was little. Of course, that was a long time ago, before everyone thought the park had become a dangerous place. Back then I used to sing along with the music. My favorite songs were "Rock-a-bye Your Baby," "Georgie Girl," and "Raindrops Keep Falling on My Head." The calliope was so loud, we couldn't even talk to each other, but it was clear from Miss Applebaum's sparkling eyes she was very much, joyously, alive. She was the most alive person I'd ever seen, waving to Henry and me on our horses. My hair crackled in the wind. But it was strange, too. I guess I had never dreamed that one day I'd end up riding a carousel with one of my teachers.

When the ride was over, Miss Applebaum jumped off her horse and called, "Hurry up! I want you to meet the Fiddler on the Hoof!"

"You mean, Fiddler on the Roof?" Henry asked.

"No—Hoof!" Miss Applebaum repeated.

Miss Applebaum darted down a promenade that was lined with snow fences set up to stop any serious drifting that might come during the winter. There were statues on both sides of us now as Miss Applebaum cried out, "Oh, there's Columbus! And there's Shakespeare! There's Robert Burns, and Einstein!" There was one genius after the other as Miss Applebaum turned from left to right with her big briefcase swinging in her hand like a bell. "That man discovered the New World! And *he* wrote *Hamlet*! And this gentleman wrote symphonies! And Schiller was one of the greatest German poets that ever lived! Aren't they wonderful!" she cried. She let out a particularly enthusiastic cry whenever she passed a scientist. "Oh, there's *Morse*! He invented the Morse Code! And there's Newton with his laws of motion! And Madame Curie with her radium! Isn't it fantastic! Doesn't it make your head spin? Just spin!"

Miss Applebaum was showing us a whole new world here that Henry and I had never really seen, even when we used to go to some of the very same parts of the park!

A statue of Mother Goose marked the beginning of another section of the park.

Miss Applebaum dashed straight onward now, right by Alice in Wonderland sitting on a toadstool and Hans Christian Andersen reading a story to a bronze duck. As usual, Henry kept his eyes glued to the ground seeing other things from his perspective such as a fallen notice about a lost dog handled by an agency called "Sherlock Bones." Farther on there was an empty bandshell. Then more hot-dog stands. Another commercial was being filmed from a van with a sign announcing "JACKIE'S LOCATION SHOOTING." Beyond that, we finally glimpsed children and full-grown men standing at the edge of a shallow pond sailing toy boats of all kinds. Most of them had sails over three feet high. There was a miniature radio-controlled tugboat. And a tiny submarine. Only two of the boats were normal small ones owned by ordinary kids.

"This is my favorite spot!" Miss Applebaum called, rushing up a grassy knoll to a bench and spinning joyously. "The Land of the Children, I call it. The Land for Children of All Ages!" At least two collies and a Schnauzer now seemed to notice Miss Applebaum, but every other living soul just seemed to be busy having fun. We heard a violin. Miss Applebaum turned. "That song is from *Camelot*!" she said happily, and we ran after her toward a man playing a violin and accompanied by a portable stereo. The man looked about ninety-seven and wore a tuxedo with a soiled frilly white shirt and fancy bowtie as though he were playing for a king. His violin case was open on the walkway in front of him, and all sorts of people and kids sat around listening and eating ice cream from a stand called the Ice Cream Cafe. Some would walk up and put a dollar in the case. Miss Applebaum kept telling us this was the famous Fiddler on the Hoof. Between numbers, Miss Applebaum hurried us up to the old man and introduced us, while he smoked a thin cigar.

"Oh, maestro, I want you to meet Henry and Zelda," she beamed, floating a dollar into his case.

"Hello," I said, smiling.

"Hello," Henry said.

"It's a pleasure to meet you," the maestro said, shaking our hands. Then, he took a big puff on his cigar and turned to Miss Applebaum. "Would you like to hear 'Tales from the Vienna Woods'?" the Fiddler on the Hoof asked.

"Oh, yes!" Miss Applebaum nodded.

As he played, Miss Applebaum had us retreat up the grassy knoll to the bench.

"Isn't it enchanting? Isn't it just enchanting?" Miss Applebaum said. "This bench! This spot! This is the most wondrous place in the world! From here, you can see everything beautiful. Everything! Do you know what I mean?" she asked.

"Yes," Henry and I said. "We know what you mean."

We had to admit this *was* the prettiest place we had ever seen in the park. Not only were there the Fiddler on the Hoof and toy boats and children catching crawfish and beautiful statues, but there were babies and rabbits and water fountains and clowns and magicians. All sorts of happy people! Other parts of the park were nice enough, but it was easy to see why here was a special place for Miss Applebaum.

"This is where all of civilization comes together

and *means* something!" Miss Applebaum exclaimed. "Where it means something important! Profound! The best of all the spirit of the world that has ever existed triumphs here and lives on," she sang out. Then she opened her briefcase and took from it a huge bag of apples. In a flash, she was on her feet running about the boat pond passing out free apples. Henry and I just sat on the bench and watched, bedazzled. It was at this moment that I happened to turn my head and notice a tremendously long ditch and a lot of construction men and machinery not very far away. They were digging a trench that looked like a very long grave, and it was headed straight toward Miss Applebaum's favorite bench. When Miss Applebaum came back, I asked her what they were doing.

"Oh, they're laying a new water pipe," she said.

"Oh," I said.

"When they finish, the park will be as good as new."

"I see," I said, but somehow the only image I could think of was a grave.

"Do you mind if Henry and I leave now?" I asked Miss Applebaum. "I told my mother I'd help her clean the house today."

"Of course," Miss Applebaum said, standing up immediately and closing her briefcase.

"We don't *really* have to go," Henry said.

"Yes, we do," I said, giving him an angry look.

"But what about the Central Park roller coaster?" Henry moaned. This time, I really *did* kick him.

"Oh, yes—we *must* go on the roller coaster," Miss Applebaum cried out, darting off.

We ran after her across a roadway and west, past another section of the construction. A wire fence had been put up, but there was one spot where we were able to go slip through and climb up a slope overlooking a large lake.

"Oh, there's the Angel of the Waters," Miss Applebaum shouted. "Isn't she beautiful?"

When we reached Miss Applebaum's side, we could see what she was talking about. There was a sign proclaiming Bethesda Terrace and a very large ornate fountain. Water squirted out at all sorts of angles from the base of a tremendous winged angel suspended by four cherubs, and all the water fell downward into a circular pool. As we hurried toward it, Miss Applebaum told us about the statue. "It is meant to be an angel who once visited a very troubled earth and brought magical waters to heal everyone. This is an angel of miracles!"

"I thought we were going to the Central Park roller coaster," Henry complained, like a complete infant.

"We are! We are!" Miss Applebaum assured him. "It's right next to the fountain!"

My heart began to beat nervously.

"I don't see a roller coaster," Henry said.

"Just hold your horses," Miss Applebaum laughed.

She marched us right past the fountain. A gentle breeze blew spray across our faces. It was cooling, and I couldn't help wishing there was a real angel on earth who had come down with a fountain of healing waters. It was a lovely, comforting thought even if it was unscientific.

Just past the fountain was a tremendous lawn sloping upward. Rosebushes were planted in formal designs. There was a rising, dazzling terrace consisting of beautiful staircases and intricately carved archways. Students sat at the edge of the lake reading. Painters worked on canvases. Photographers snapped away. There were beds of late-blooming marigolds. Miss Applebaum rushed up the stairs on one side. "Here's the roller coaster!" she called out to us. "Here's where you get on!"

I looked at Henry and I could see even he was worried now that the moment was at hand.

At the top of the stairs, Miss Applebaum darted out onto the lawn. We followed her, and by the time we reached her, she was sitting on the grass and had set her hat and briefcase on a stump.

"Hurry! Lie down! The roller coaster's about to leave. Hurry!"

It was crazy, but Henry made me do as she said. All we were doing was sitting on top of a grass hill overlooking the great fountain.

"Don't we need a ticket?" Henry asked.

"No!" Miss Applebaum shouted, stretching herself out.

"Miss Applebaum . . ." I tried to speak, but couldn't quite find words.

"Here we go!" she cried.

And then she did it.

She began to roll.

She rolled and she rolled and she rolled. And I heard her laugh. She laughed as she rolled over and over and over.

And then Henry began to roll after her, shouting to me, “Come on! Come on!”

So then I started rolling.

It was only seconds before all three of us were rolling and laughing, rolling down, down, down on the Central Park roller coaster.

Chapter Seven

I don't agree with everything Zelda said about Central Park; therefore, I'm drawing a map so I can introduce more of a reality factor. Reality factors have always been my job when Zelda *sublimates* and tries to paint anything better than it really is. It was a unique experience, having Miss Applebaum show us her statuary and favorite botanic haunts, but it's my duty to put things into better perspective. These additional reality factors are: 1) Zelda told you I was wearing a wacky sweatshirt, but she didn't tell you she was wearing a blue suit jacket with six pieces of gaudy costume jewelry stuck on it. She wears so much jewelry, you'd think she was always opening at Radio City Music Hall. 2) By the time we had left Central Park, Zelda let Miss Applebaum buy her one Milk Duds, one Fresca lemon soda, and a frozen chocolate-covered banana. It wasn't that she was taking advantage of Miss Applebaum, but Miss Applebaum insisted. Besides my first Fudgsicle I had one salted pretzel, one Clark bar, a second Fudgsicle, and a small Sugar Daddy. I mean, Miss Applebaum just pushed the stuff on us. We saw Miss Applebaum beginning to wheeze again, so we let her buy us the stuff so she could rest while we ate. Also, when we left Miss Applebaum in front of her apartment house, she mentioned Dr. Obitcheck was coming over in the afternoon to give her another treatment, and we knew what that meant.

Zelda and I went to school on Monday, and it was strange that neither one of us mentioned Miss Applebaum. Zelda would explain that phenomenon by saying that we had "thanatophobia," which means "the fear of death." Zelda loves the word "thanatophobia" and the only reason I learned it was because she uses it in almost every book report she writes. But Zelda and I each have a different kind of fear about the Grim Reaper. For the most part, Zelda is worried about the regular death that happens when you grow too old. I'm worried about death coming in more unique ways, but I don't let it really hang me up. For instance, my worst fear is that when I'm walking down a street someone's Crazy Eddie air conditioner is going to fall on me. Other falling objects I watch out for are large cranes, bricks, planks, pianos, and pennies. Some kid once told me that if someone threw a penny off a thirty-story building, it would gain enough speed to sink four inches into a passerby's brain. There are other passing thoughts of danger I have, such as keeping an eye out every time I pass a sewer. A lot of kids I know go to visit Disneyland in Florida and come back with baby alligators, and then they get bored with them and flush them down their toilets. Also, some people lose their pet pythons and iguanas and you never know what drainpipe they're going to pop out of. I've never told this

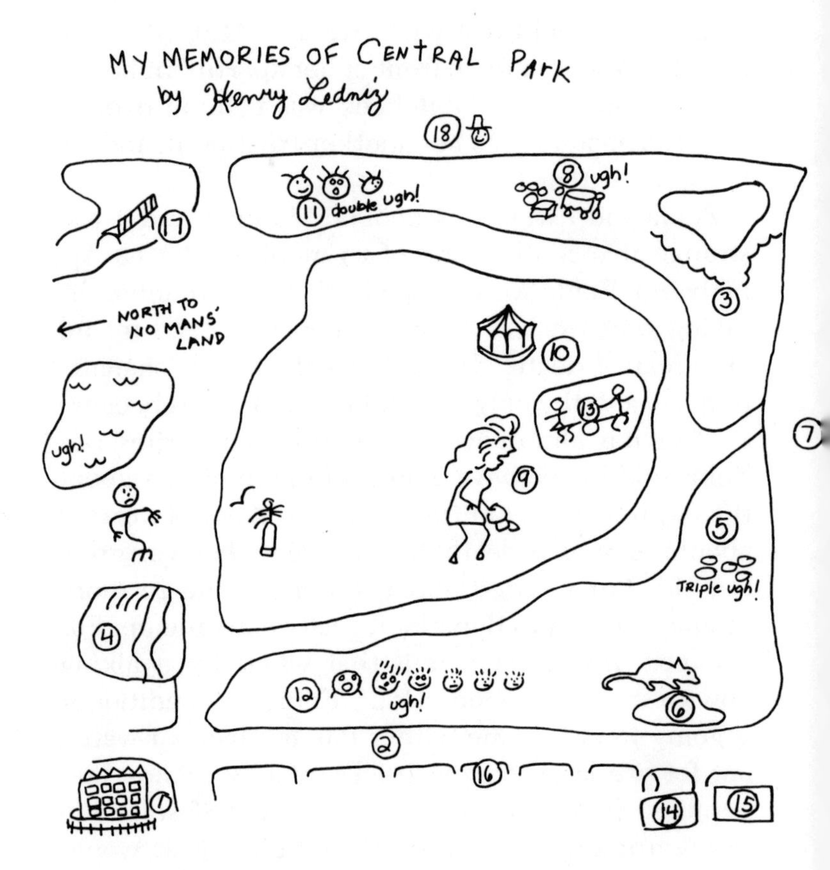

1 The Dakota where John Lennon was shot
2 Central Park West
3 Most drug sellers
4 Daniel Webster statue
5 Most dog waste
6 Most rats on one rock
7 Central Park South
8 Most garbage
9 Cops dressed as women
10 Boring carousel
11 Most muggers
12 Most bums
13 Ugliest playground
14 Zelda's apartment
15 My apartment
16 Miss Applebaum's place
17 Miss Applebaum's favorite bench
18 Fifth Avenue snobs

to anyone before, but sometimes just before I go to sleep I wonder if when I die, I should be cremated or buried in a casket. The one thing I know is, I don't want to be sealed up in an ornate urn or have my body preserved in a cement crypt like Nat King Cole or Marilyn Monroe. I hate all those modern high-rise cemeteries with all the bodies stacked in cubicles due to escalating real estate prices. It's bad enough that we have to live in fairly small apartments when we're alive. And I have very special feelings about what I want my casket made of, if I don't choose to go up in smoke. I want it made of the cheapest wood so that it will disintegrate as fast as possible. I have this theory that the sooner all my atoms are released back into the world, then the sooner I will drift around and become parts of other living things. Parts of me could end up in raspberry bushes, trout streams, weeping willow trees, and all sorts of pleasant things. I could be swallowed by energetic fish and munched on by good-natured cows and other domestic animals and then start moving all over the place in unusual bloodstreams and lymph nodes. Eventually, I could be transferred over great distances and become part of steaks and vegetables eaten by people in Westchester, Liverpool, or Bombay. My atoms could be bounced and transformed by bald eagles and munching children and chirping chickens and devout priests. I could become part of famous governors, brilliant writers, and benevolent presidents. I could drift to the moon and Uranus and back again! Sometimes, after I've drifted off to sleep, I even dream that all my atoms and molecules eventually could meet up with each other again in the exact combination of the original sperm and egg that made me, and then Henry Maximilian Ledniz would be born again. Which is as good a time as any to tell you about my berserk parents.

As I already told you, my mother is the Freudian Octopus and my father is the Cockaloony Bird. My mother has her psychoanalytic practice in an office in 26G in the same building where we live. She sees all her patients there. The only thing is, is that my mother is nuttier than any of her patients, so I can't believe people actually pay money for her to treat them. And my father is one of the most self-centered people I've ever known. Actually, both my parents are only really interested in themselves. It's the Eighth Wonder of the World they ever got together enough to have me. The Freudian Octopus hides out in her office all day and the Cockaloony Bird is constantly commuting to Princeton, where he teaches equations whenever he has to. Usually, he tells us about how engrossed he is in reading the latest mystery novel like *Death Wore Pantyhose*, and he stops at New Jersey Turnpike rest areas to devour whole chapters. My parents *look* weird, too. My mother looks like a matron of a concentration camp who uses an ax to shear her own hair, and my father bears a striking resemblance to Vincent van Gogh. They both waited until late in life to have me, and I think they mated by appointment. They do all human activity by appointment. Even Zelda says they are the most structured people she's ever known, but I've learned how to work around that by now. For instance, I suspected I was going to need a lot of free time to be able to go over and see Miss Applebaum whenever I felt like it. Zelda's parents are understanding about charitable human wishes like that, but I had to go about matters slightly differently. It took me until Wednesday at dinner before I could really set things up.

"Eat your moo goo gai pan," the Freudian Octopus said, opening up a packet of soy sauce.

We have Chinese or Italian food delivered twenty or thirty times a month because my mother and father think cooking inhibits their professional lives.

"Did you order enough mu shu pork pancakes?" the Cockaloony Bird wanted to know.

"I ordered eight," the Octopus said proudly, "so there'll be two left over for lunch. Only four came with the order and each of the other pancakes was fifty cents." She ran her fingers through her buzz-cut hairdo.

"How's your math this term?" Cockaloony wanted to know.

"Fine," I said.

"I think we should get you a tutor." Octopus munched, squeezing hot mustard all over her food.

"I don't need a tutor."

"Oh, you say you don't need a tutor, but when the college entrance exams come around, you'll be grateful we insisted on extra preparation," Octopus said. "I've set up the first part of your after-school schedule. Mondays you have the Greek tutor, Tuesdays you have chess, Wednesdays you have tennis and Latin. You know, Henry Maximilian, I signed you up to take a test for Columbia. If you pass it, you'll be eligible for their high school accelerated program for gifted students."

"I'm not gifted, Mom," I mumbled, trying to pull out all the pieces of shrimp in my egg roll that looked like they were laundered in Haiti.

Octopus and Cockaloony don't really listen to me, so it didn't matter what I said. They just kept digging into their fried dumplings and twisted noodles.

"What are you reading now?" the Octopus asked the Cockaloony Bird without really looking at him. Sometimes, my parents mechanically play husband and wife, and it's so phony I just sit back and listen like I'm at a play.

"Hell House."

"Sounds interesting."

"I can't put it down."

"You know, I really think the moo goo gai pan is better at Madame Wu's."

"It's about a scientist whose chimpanzees become smarter than him thanks to a computer. The biogenetic implications are completely credible."

"I have a new patient who is a computer analyst," the Octopus said, stabbing a black mushroom with a fork. She looked like she was nibbling on a monkey's ear.

"The author seems to really know his math, and the chimps are truly haunting."

"My patient has nightmares about being shredded.

Every night, he wakes up screaming that machinery is stalking him. His lover is completely distraught."

"Most of the plot revolves around an ape's knowledge of calculus. The pacing's much better than in *Kiss of the Covenant.*"

The Octopus and Cockaloony Bird sometimes talk like that for fifteen minutes before they remember I'm still in the room. It was a mistake for them to have me, but I really don't blame them for it. They both come from generations of insensitive and cold families, so when Zelda recorded that I sometimes have trouble expressing my real feelings, I think she was right. No feelings are exhibited in my family. Everything is done by the numbers, including the expression of my parents' guilt. Zelda helped me understand a long time ago that my parents feel so guilty about not having the ability to really love me, that they sign me up for endless extracurricular activities to keep me out of the house. I was the youngest kid in my grammar school to be sent away to all-summer sleep-away camps. I've gone to camps that specialize in almost every subject. I've gone to geology camps. My father even once found an advanced algebra camp. They've never known what to do with me after school, so they've signed me up for lessons in German, soccer, choir, piano, violin, squash, music appreciation, karate, pottery, horseback-riding, kite flying, and origami. They booked me so solid out of their guilt that I almost had twenty nervous breakdowns, but I caught on to them by the time I was eleven. And once I caught on to their problem, I found it easy to short-circuit them. I used to sit back and they'd book me solid so I didn't have a spare minute during a schoolday or weekend. Now, I just beat them at their own game.

"A teacher from school is starting a weekend seminar in science," I said.

The Octopus stopped chewing on a fortune cookie and actually looked at me, her eyes bulging with true interest for a second.

"That's wonderful!" she said.

"Terrific," Cockaloony agreed, slipping *Hell House* onto the table and starting to read.

"Who?" Octopus actually wanted to know. "What teacher?"

"Miss Applebaum. I really would like to study with her," I added. I knew they never remember anything about my teachers, so I could have mentioned someone who got hit by a subway last year and they wouldn't have known.

"Of course," Cockaloony said, sounding a bit like he'd just O.D.'d on monosodium glutamate. A bean sprout clung to his lower lip like a larva.

"It's an intensive course."

"How many weekends?" Octopus asked hopefully.

"Lots."

"Great. What's the name of the course?"

"The Flora and Fauna of Central Park."

"It sounds fascinating," Cockaloony mumbled as he moved himself into a Panasonic stereophonic massage chair with a vibrating ottoman.

"There'll be a lot of sleep-over events," I added temptingly.

Octopus said, "I'll write a check immediately. How much is it?"

"Twenty dollars per weekend."

"Isn't that cheap?"

"Yes. It's subsidized."

"Do I just make the check payable to Miss Applebaum?"

"*Cash.* She wants just cash," I stressed.

"Now, that's what I call a smart teacher," the Octopus said as I cracked my fortune cookie. "Beat the IRS whenever you can. What does your fortune say?" She glanced at her watch and continued nonstop. "You know, I have a manic depressive due upstairs in twenty minutes. We'll have pizza tomorrow night. Here's a hundred for five weeks."

In a moment the Cockaloony Bird was snoring and the Freudian Octopus was gone.

I read my fortune to myself.

"CONFUCIUS SAY THERE IS NO CURE
FOR LOVE OR DEATH."

"Would you like first to learn the game Goonie, or should we play Elevator Roulette, or perhaps make exploding hydrogen balloons?" Miss Applebaum asked, smiling at us.

"I vote for the exploding hydrogen balloons," I said.

"Do you think we should?" Zelda asked.

"Of course," Miss Applebaum insisted.

It had taken me straight up to Saturday afternoon before I could get Zelda to return to Miss Applebaum's apartment. Thanks to my parents, I was better financed this time, so we brought her the biggest blooming begonia plant they had at Ye Green Thumb and a box of imported Amaretti's chocolate oysters. Amaretti's chocolate oysters aren't real oysters; they're just made in the shape of oysters. And we even called Miss Applebaum before we went over. You should have heard how happy she sounded to hear from us, and she wasn't wheezing at all.

Miss Applebaum went around the apartment selecting all sorts of apparatus. Zelda sat nervously on the wicker sofa while I followed Miss Applebaum, weaving in and out of all the split-leaf philodendrons, around the flower Ferris wheel, and past the stuffed alligator and the huge model of the human ear.

"Here's a piece of string, a glass bottle, and a balloon—and of course we'll have a carbon dioxide fire extinguisher on hand just in case," Miss Applebaum said excitedly.

Before we could say "Bingo," Miss Applebaum had the balloon on a one-hole stopper attached to a bottle that had a little zinc and sulfuric acid bubbling away in it.

"Maybe we shouldn't," Zelda said.

"Of course we should," I said.

"It's perfectly safe," Miss Applebaum assured Zelda. The balloon filled with hydrogen. Then, Miss Applebaum tied the end of the balloon with a string fuse and let it rise to the ceiling.

"Can I light it?" I begged.

"Of course. Just strike the match away from you," Miss Applebaum instructed.

"*Don't*, Henry," Zelda whispered.
I lit the bottom of the string.

I mean, it wasn't exactly an explosion like the Hindenburg blimp, but it was a modestly entertaining *Kaboom!* And it loosened Zelda up, because then even she wanted to perform a bevy of other experiments Miss Applebaum suggested. We made a litmus fountain by heating an Erlenmeyer flask with a butane cylinder burner. Of course, Miss Applebaum carefully supervised anything that required heat. Then we made a very powerful electromagnet by wrapping a thousand turns of insulated wire around a big bolt and marched around the apartment picking up various metal objects, such as paperweights, staple guns, and a transistor radio. Miss Applebaum even got the wind tunnel going for us, and we peered at onion tissue under one of the antique microscopes. The equipment was old, but it still worked. We also took apart the giant flower model and wired a telegraph system so Zelda could tap out messages from the living room all the way down the hall to me in Miss Applebaum's bedroom. Of course, Miss Applebaum's bedroom was filled with a lot of scientific equipment, but there were also stacks of clothing, worn hatboxes, well-traveled suitcases, and approximately another hundred potted representatives of the vegetable kingdom.

When we got tired of experimentation, Miss Applebaum brewed authentic Ceylonese tea in a beautiful painted clay pot, and we sat back on the wicker with delicate cups in our hands like refined English gentry.

"Are you sure you've never played Goonie?" Miss Applebaum inquired.

"I'm sure," I said.

"It's something we would remember," Zelda assured her.

Miss Applebaum laughed and rushed to a desk drawer. She pulled out a deck of cards and sat in a very ladylike manner on the floor in front of the coffee table. She dealt everyone four cards, which we picked up for our eyes only. Then Miss Applebaum put the rest of the pack down and started lifting up one card at a time. She'd check each card to see if she needed it to make a match with whatever she had in her hand and, if she couldn't use it, she just passed it along clockwise.

"You see, you try to get four cards the same, such as four fives, or four eights, or four Jacks, or four of anything!" she explained.

"*Then* what?" I asked.

"Well, the first person to get four of a kind sticks their tongue out just a tiny bit."

"Their tongue out?"

"Yes," Miss Applebaum chuckled. "But you keep shoving the cards along as though nothing has happened until a *second* player notices you have your tongue out, and then he or she sticks *her* tongue out! That leaves only a third person, who's the last to catch on, so the first two with their tongues out point at him and yell, 'Goonie!' The last one to stick their tongue out gets the first letter *G.* And then the next person deals, and we keep playing until someone has lost six times, and then he or she is the *whole* 'Goonie'! Get it?"

"Oh, yes, we get it," Zelda said.

"Yes," I agreed, thinking how remarkable it was that Miss Applebaum could switch from serious experiments to silly games, and enjoy both!

It sounded slightly berserk, but before we knew it, we were all dealing like crazy and getting cockeyed, keeping one eye on our cards and the other to see if anyone was sticking out a tongue before the others. It really turned out to be a terrific diversion, and we ended up playing twenty-three games. We started yelling "Goonie" as though our lives depended upon it, and we laughed and rolled on the floor until our sides ached. I must say I never thought in a trillion years I'd be playing Goonie with one of my retired schoolteachers. It was unique the way Miss Applebaum shared everything with us. We sent out for a Ray's Original pizza with sausage and anchovies. And Miss Applebaum didn't breathe funny at all during any of the explosions, card playing, or tea sipping. I mean, we went at it until we had to put the lights on in the apartment because it had gotten dark outside. Then we made cinnamon buns, and after that, we defrosted a Sara Lee German chocolate cake. Just before eight o'clock, Miss Applebaum insisted we top the whole thing off with big bowls of Jell-O Instant vanilla pudding with Häagen-Dazs rum raisin ice cream. I know that was about eight P.M. because Zelda had also called her mother to tell her she and I were dining out, and that Zelda would be home a little late. Of course, I *didn't* have to call the

Freudian Octopus or the Cockaloony Bird. I would have gotten their answering machine anyway.

Everything was going peachy-dory at Miss Applebaum's the whole night until around seven minutes to nine. That was when Zelda and I met one of the meanest persons we'd ever met. What happened was that Miss Applebaum got around to teaching us how to play Elevator Roulette. What we had to do was go out into the hall and then take turns standing in front of the closed elevator door. Miss Applebaum went first to demonstrate, while Zelda and I stood to one side.

"Now, I press the call button," Miss Applebaum explained, "and when the elevator comes, I make a fright face like *this*!"

Miss Applebaum suddenly sucked in her lower lip, puckered her upper one, and opened her eyes as wide as saucers. The face she made had Zelda and me laughing our heads off as the elevator headed for our floor, but when the door opened, nobody was in it.

"See?" Miss Applebaum relaxed. "That's Elevator Roulette. If the door opens and nobody's in it, you get only one point. But if the door opens and someone's in it to see you making a funny face, well, then you get five points! And the first one to get fifty points wins!"

I went next, and I stuck one finger in my mouth to pull my left lip down so I looked like a demented aardvark. Then I pressed the button for the elevator and, when it came, nobody was in it again, so I only got one point. Then Zelda went, and she pulled her hair over the front of her face and hunched over so she looked like a hairy blob. This time when the elevator came, there was an old man in it with a Persian cat. Both of them were completely freaked out by the sight of Zelda, and me and Miss Applebaum practically collapsed laughing. That gave Zelda five points right off. During the next fifteen minutes, we got to shock a lot of people because around that time people in apartment houses take their assorted pets out for walks. I frightened two airline stewardesses, one lady with a bulldog, one man delivering a deli sandwich, and a guy with a bike. Besides the old man and the Persian cat, Zelda shocked three businessmen and a baby-sitter. Miss Applebaum frightened a visiting nurse, a lady with blue hair, and a Chinese man with a Lhasa Apso. When we saw their faces, we laughed and laughed and laughed, and sometimes the persons in the elevator laughed, too. What finally happened was we started playing Elevator Roulette with first two of us making funny faces, and then we made it all three of us.

"Isn't this fun?" Miss Applebaum cried.

"Yes!" Zelda and I agreed.

I even started standing on my head, and Miss Applebaum and Zelda would each hold one of my legs. In less than five minutes, we had discombobulated a rabbi, two old men carrying a checkerboard, and a professional dog walker. We were so delirious, we could no longer keep track of our scores, and we were on one of our worst laughing jags, doing the cancan and rolling our eyes up into the back of our heads, when the elevator door opened with a lady inside, and Zelda and I knew the game was over.

"Aunt Alice!" the woman said to Miss Applebaum in a chilling, disciplinarian voice.

"Oh, *Bernice*," Miss Applebaum sputtered. We all stopped doing high kicks and stared.

"Just what is going on here?" the woman demanded, stepping off the elevator.

"We were just playing a game," Miss Applebaum said innocently.

"Who is this?" the woman asked, indicating Zelda and me as though we were a single unit of worthlessness.

"My friends," Miss Applebaum said. "Henry and Zelda. They were in my class, and they worked for me and—"

"I see," the woman interrupted. "If you don't mind, we'll go inside." She stormed straight for the open door to Miss Applebaum's apartment.

"This is my niece, Bernice," Miss Applebaum said, trying to introduce her.

In a moment we were all back inside Miss Applebaum's apartment, and Bernice was casing the joint. She seemed to look particularly at the scattered playing cards on the coffee table, the pile of cups, saucers, the pizza box, and the empty Sara Lee aluminum tray.

"We were having a little fun," Miss Applebaum explained.

"Yes, you *were*," Bernice said.

Zelda and I were surprised to see Miss Applebaum had a fairly old niece. Most of the time when we get introduced to someone's niece, it's somebody slightly young. I just never usually think about the fact that nieces get older, too. And nieces are supposed to be demure and nice, but this Bernice was not. She had a face like a buzz saw, with fancy, dyed, stiff blond hair, and she spoke precise English as though she had been born to a manor near Loch Ness. She was excessively statuesque with a diamond ring. She thought she was hot stuff.

"Aunt Alice, go lie down," Bernice ordered.

"I'm not tired," Miss Applebaum said, sounding a bit intimidated herself. It was as though Miss Applebaum was the niece and Bernice was the aunt.

"I said, 'Go lie down.' "

"But Zelda and Henry and I were—"

"They're going home," Bernice said flatly.

"But—"

"We *do* have to leave," Zelda spoke up. We didn't want to make any more trouble for Miss Applebaum.

"I'll just see them to the elevator," Miss Applebaum said.

"No, you won't see them anywhere," Bernice informed her. "*I* will."

"'Bye," Zelda and I said quickly to Miss Applebaum.

Zelda grabbed her jacket quickly, and I my sweater. I didn't even wait to put it on.

"Please come again," Miss Applebaum practically pleaded.

Bernice gave us the bum's rush out the door, and followed us out closing the apartment door behind her. Bernice stalked us to the elevator, took control of the call button, and spun to face us like a dragoness.

"Your aunt was our teacher," we tried to explain.

"The operative word is *was*," Bernice stressed, using the most caustic whisper tones I'd ever heard. In the harsh light of the hallway, I could see she spent hours plucking her eyebrows into tiny crescent slivers, and painted her witch-long fingernails blood red. She looked like she spent a fortune on makeup, and she was forty years old if she was a day.

"You know my aunt is ill," Bernice zeroed in.

"Yes—" Zelda sputtered.

"*How* do you know?"

"We heard."

"*How* did you hear?"

"We heard at school that she was ill."

"How ill do you think she is?"

"Very ill," Zelda said, and I could see she was ready to cry.

"That's correct. She is *very* ill; she is *dying*," Bernice whispered ruthlessly. "And do you think you should be coming over here bothering an old dying woman? Do you think that's very nice?"

"We love her," Zelda said.

"Let's just get something straight. I never want you to come over here again. You keep away from her!"

"We all enjoy being together. She does too!"

"She has only *months* to live," Bernice shot at me.

"Says who? That cockeyed doctor from Weehawken?" I growled back at her. I could tell I threw her off balance.

"You met Dr. Obitcheck?" Bernice wanted to know. *"How?"*

"We were here once when he came. We brought Miss Applebaum a begonia," I said.

"Then you know she needs more than flowers!" Bernice pressed the call button viciously.

"Why can't she be treated? Why can't anyone do anything?" Zelda asked.

"I'll tell you why," Bernice shouted, and then dropped her voice back into a snakelike hiss. "Because her illness has spread too far in her body. It's in the lining of her lungs and in her lymph system. She's riddled with it. There's nothing you or I or any doctor on earth can do to save her."

The elevator arrived, and Zelda and I walked onto it. Bernice reached out and held back the door, stopping it from closing.

"Can't we at least come see her?" Zelda asked.

"No. I'm here at least once a week. Soon there'll be a visiting nurse. *I don't want her to know she's dying.*"

We gasped.

"Are you saying Miss Applebaum doesn't *know*?" Zelda cried.

"She doesn't want to know!" Bernice practically screamed at us. "She *and* I don't want you ruining whatever few months she has left."

"She seemed to be happy seeing us," I said.

The elevator door started to slam against Bernice's hand, making a terrible racket. It grew louder and began thumping like a heartbeat.

"Look, I want you out of here," Bernice shot at us.

"And if I ever hear that you so much as come near my aunt again, you'll be sorry! Just let my aunt die in peace!"

She yanked her hand away and the elevator door closed like the lid on a nightmare.

Chapter Eight

As Henry and I told you in the beginning, there will be no lies in this book. Therefore, it is my duty to tell you that we both intensely hated Bernice. There are very few persons in the world we don't like, but Miss Applebaum's niece was on the top of the list. Almost all the others we can't stand are ayatollahs, politicians, or malevolent despots, and some of them aren't even alive anymore, but we hate them in retrospect. Henry and I tried to consider every possible psychological motive Bernice could have for not telling her own aunt that she was dying, but we didn't arrive at even a clue. In fact, meeting Bernice so traumatized me that I had nightmares all week. In one nightmare I was a supernumerary in *La Bohème* again, one of the children dancing around the toymaster when a major diva is rolled onstage in a carriage. In my dream this major diva turned out to have the chilling face of Bernice, and she suddenly commanded an entire regiment to guillotine Henry and me while she sang "Musetta's Waltz." It was a very disturbing nightmare, and I woke up screaming. Later the same night, I dreamed Bernice buried me alive, which I found very symbolic from a Freudian point of view. I think it represented Bernice's desire to suppress anyone who might want to help Miss Applebaum. I can only tell you the facts as I remember them, but I do recall my own powers of repression were in high gear all through this period. As it turned out, this was to be the week in which Henry and I made one of the decisions that may haunt us forever.

Henry called me night and day and I tried to avoid the obvious issue, but he finally dragged me to the Cosmic Soda Shoppe on Tuesday A.B. (we'd come to define time as "After Bernice"). He at least waited until after Large Marge had brought us our frozen hot chocolates before he began to railroad me into a discussion I didn't feel ready to have.

"We have to tell Miss Applebaum," Henry said.

"No, we don't."

I knew Henry wasn't completely sure of what he was saying, because he kept excessively turning to see if a taxi or bus was going to veer onto the sidewalk and crash into our booth.

"We *do* have to tell her!"

"No, we don't!" And then, "Besides, maybe Miss Applebaum already has it all figured out herself," I muttered.

Of course, I wasn't sure of anything I was saying either. Henry and I had already had practically the same argument fifty times on street corners and between classes. It wasn't that we didn't have enough to keep us busy with full programs in English, biology, early American history, French, algebra, and Introduction to Family Living. What we did *not* do was sign up to work as lab assistants for service credits. It would only have reminded us of Miss Applebaum and how worried we were for her.

By Thursday, I still hadn't committed myself to anything, and I went home alone instead of going out with Henry again. My mother came home from her guidance counselor job at four-fifteen. She took one look at my face and knew she'd have a little home counseling to do.

"What's the matter?" she asked.

"Nothing."

"Zeldaaaaaaaaaaaa!" she said, with the inflection that always signals she knows I knew more than I'm saying. "It's something about Miss Applebaum, isn't it?" She hit the nail on the head.

"Yes."

"Well, shoot."

My mom shoved a roll of Scott paper towels and a can of Lemon Pledge in my hands. She pointed me toward the dining room table. Everytime my mom wants to draw me out on a problem, she gets me to do something domestic. I think she instinctively knows it's easier for me to talk if I'm doing something physical and mundane, which just happens also to be a technique of Stanislavski, the famous, deceased acting teacher. I told her about meeting Miss Applebaum's niece.

"I hear she's a beaut," my mother said, running her hand through her perm.

"You know about her?" I asked with surprise.

"I've *heard* about her."

"From whom?"

"Her name comes up a lot. I had another coffee schmooze with Helen Kaminski, the nurse at my school, and she always hears everything directly from Mr. Kennedy at Andrew Jackson. Kaminski and Kennedy were at a Rollo May lecture at Ethical Culture, and he told her Miss Applebaum's niece had taken complete charge of filing the retirement forms last June, and that it's not the first time the niece has moved in on Miss Applebaum's affairs. I hear she's a witch on wheels."

"Is it possible Miss Applebaum doesn't know she's dying? Is that something her niece and her doctor and everyone could just keep from her?"

"Nothing would surprise me," my mother said, taking a damp sponge and starting to wipe the dining room chair cushions. "By the way, I got student discount tickets for a musical version of *How Green Was My Valley*," she added. "You and Henry may want to go, but I hope they don't have a tap-dancing wheat field or anything like that."

"No thanks, Mom."

"There's something else, isn't there?" she asked, giving her sponge a rinse.

I pressed the nozzle on the Lemon Pledge can and hid behind a spray of mist for a moment.

"I just don't know why her niece doesn't want her to know everything," I finally said. "If I were going to die, I'd want to know. There'd be things I'd want to take care of."

"They say the niece lives in a house she bought with a loan from Miss Applebaum's pension fund last year. Some families do very strange things when someone's sick. They fight over money. Connive. They stick their grandmothers in nursing homes. Put them on charity. Helen Kaminski said Applebaum's niece married an alcoholic real estate agent and they live in a Westport colonial they can't afford. I hear the niece has taken advantage of Miss Applebaum for years."

That's when it came to me that maybe Bernice wasn't trying to protect her aunt from knowing about her dying out of kindness to her. She didn't want her to know so she'd die sooner, and her money would go to Bernice!

I realize I'm very lucky to have a mother and father I can talk to, but I suppose I have to admit here and now that there are some things I really don't feel comfortable telling them. I don't talk to them about my very deepest feelings. I don't know how to express those to them, and in some strange way I don't think I really should. I really want to discuss the most secret parts of my mind and heart only with Henry. I guess practically all the secret parts we share have to do with God, love, sex, and death, and a lot of those feelings and thoughts we have trouble putting into words even for ourselves. Henry already mentioned his phobias, but he doesn't let them interfere with his life. If he has an anxiety attack, he's so brave no one can tell there's anything bothering him. I can tell because when he's frightened, his cowlick stands straight up on his head. I think it has something to do with his forehead muscles. When I'm scared, I start to cry. Henry makes it sound as if my tear ducts open up like floodgates, but my eyes really only become red and moist. Rarely do actual tears roll down my cheeks.

My fears about dying *are* different than Henry's. I usually don't think about death unless something in my environment triggers it, such as passing a graveyard or Riverside Funeral Parlor. To me, death is unfair. It is so unfair that I almost go crazy whenever I really think about it. And my fears about death are very sensible ones, I believe. They are questions to which I have no answers. I think death is the most horrible thing inflicted on the human race. I can't stand it. I don't want it to exist. It's the most horrible thing about being born. And I don't know what to think about God. I used to believe in one. I still try to start each day not thinking about anything connected to my future personal extinction, but it's very difficult. And the terrifying things that were to happen to me, Henry, and Miss Applebaum are different and more disturbing than anything I've ever seen on TV. On television whenever some delicate old lady or beloved person is going to die, they always find a lot of hope at the end by cutting to newborn babies, puppies, or a marriage ceremony. It's all so fake. It frightens me because we are bombarded by electronic lies, and the only thing that scares me more than all the lies about life is what statistics indicate are the truth about life. Henry and I never meet religious people. Most kids Henry and I know don't feel like praying to a force that kills them. I think millions and millions of human beings are in a terrible crisis. I once read in a psychology article that most people have gone insane because to *not* be insane would just be another form of insanity. I think that's what happened to Henry's parents, if you ask me. He calls his mother the Freudian Octopus, but a lot of people admire the way she is a woman with a highly respected career. I don't think she means to be an incompetent mother, but being a psychoanalyst must make her think all day about the thousands of problems of being alive. Psychoanalysts think about those problems all day long, so it's no accident Mrs. Ledniz belongs to an occupation with the highest rate of suicide, second only to dentists. I heard on the news once that a married pair of psychoanalysts committed a double suicide last winter on an ice floe. And Henry's father is much more than a Cockaloony Bird. My father told me many people once knew him as a very respected mathematician, and that it's only lately he's escaped into reading multitudinous mystery novels. My mother also says he's undergoing male menopause. He just waited too long in life to get married and conceive Henry. Whatever, I do think both Mr. and Mrs. Ledniz both deserve respect and understanding, and I believe Henry does love them no matter what he says. Whatever, this fear of death both Henry and I have must be one of the things that makes us such good friends. And maybe it was this fear that took us a full six days to decide that we absolutely had to tell Miss Applebaum she was going to die.

It was after school on that Friday afternoon I told Henry my theory about Bernice and we finally called Miss Applebaum. Henry and I were alone at the Ledniz main apartment, and after he dialed I picked up the living room extension.

"Hello," Miss Applebaum answered.

"Hi," Henry said. "It's Henry and Zelda, Miss Applebaum."

"Oh, I've been waiting for your call," Miss Applebaum said right away. She sounded desperately happy to hear from us.

"We were wondering if we could see you," I said.

"Of course! I've already planned our whole trip to the museum!"

"The museum?"

"Yes! The museum! I insist on taking you both to the museum. Can we go tomorrow? Can we? Please?"

"Yes," Henry said.

"What about your niece?" I asked. "Will your niece be coming over?"

"Oh, no," Miss Applebaum assured me. "Besides, Bernice isn't half as much a spoilsport as she sometimes seems."

"I'm sure," Henry said.

As it turned out, the museum she was talking about was the Metropolitan Museum, all the way to the east side of Central Park, which is the museum Henry and I go to the least. Most of our homework assignments and class trips are centered around the museum on the west side, where we live. We offered to stop by and pick Miss Applebaum up, but she suggested we just meet her at the West 72nd Street entrance like we did the first time. Of course, it didn't really matter where Miss Applebaum wanted to take us, because Henry and I knew that before the day was out, we'd have to make certain she knew she was dying. That has to be the hardest thing any human being has to tell another.

Henry and I arrived at the park entrance ten minutes early. It was a sunny, very cold day, and we both wore sweaters and denim jackets as we sat on a bench directly across from where Lucifer's baby was born in fiction and John Lennon was murdered in reality. I wore only a large rhinestone green turtle pin on my lapel and Henry wore a large button that said SCHIZOPHRENIA BEATS BEING ALONE. At 10:05 A.M., we saw Miss Applebaum and her black homburg hat come marching out of a delicatessen down from the Dakota. The moment she saw us, she was smiling and waving again, and hurried toward us. She was wearing a mouton lamb coat we had seen her wear to Andrew Jackson High all last winter, but it wasn't buttoned, so it flapped in the breeze. Actually, everything she was wearing was familiar and she was again carrying her big leather briefcase we had always seen her lug up to the third floor lab. At first she looked quite energetic, but by the time she started to cross the street, she appeared to run a little out of steam. When she reached us, she was actually puffing like the night we had first visited her, but it didn't seem to interfere with her joy at meeting us.

"Hello, hello, hello!" Miss Applebaum beamed as her eyes lit up under her hat.

"Let me hold your briefcase for you," Henry offered, and I could tell he was worried about her, too.

"I'm fine," Miss Applebaum said.

"No, please let me," Henry insisted, taking the briefcase.

"Well, maybe you could just hold it," Miss Applebaum agreed. "Then I can give Helen her coffee," she added, opening the catch.

Henry and I stared down into the satchel. It was filled with dozens of containers of coffee and a lot of Entenmeyer donuts.

"Where's Helen?" I asked.

"There!" Miss Applebaum pointed to a pile of newspapers and Hefty Bags *under* a bench. "Breakfast time, Helen! Breakfast time!"

This time, I took one of the coffees and a donut and set them down on a napkin near one end of the newspapers. A withered hand crept out, grasped the food, and disappeared again.

"'Bye, Helen," Miss Applebaum sang, and in a flash we were off into the park.

"I have twenty-six coffees and powdered donuts today," Miss Applebaum specified, still puffing.

"Maybe we shouldn't walk so fast," I suggested.

"Why not?" Miss Applebaum wanted to know.

"I sprained my ankle a little," Henry lied. Miss Applebaum looked at him as though she knew he was lying, but Henry added, "Besides, you don't want to spill any of the coffee. You know, sometimes containers open or crack, and things like that."

"Oh, children," Miss Applebaum sang out, "did you know that the donut is a geometrical wonder? Did you know that?"

"No, we didn't."

"Oh, but it is!" Miss Applebaum insisted. "The humble donut is part of a whole new theory of the cosmos! A whole new theory of the universe based on the discovery that the laws concerning the surface area of a donut are exactly the same as the laws concerning the shape of a cup," she declared happily. "Here, let me demonstrate."

Miss Applebaum dashed onto a horse path, picked up a stick, and began drawing in the dirt.

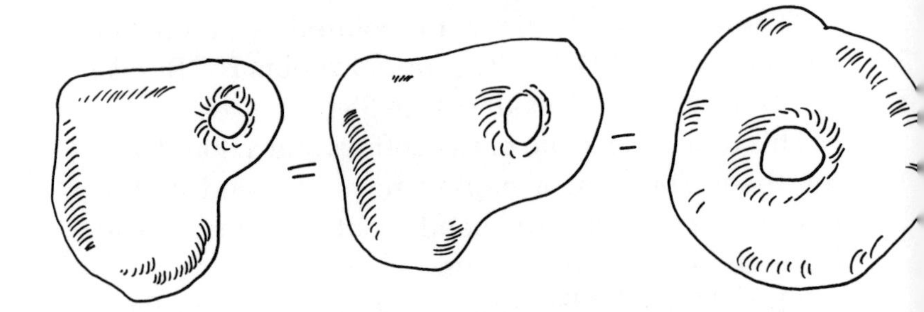

"See? A cup has the same dimensional qualities as a donut! Isn't that marvelous! Do you see how daring it is for a scientist to even discover that fact? How unique his or her mind had to be?" Miss Applebaum asked.

"Yes."

"So much of life depends completely on how you look at it," she chirped. "Imagine! A whole new idea about the galaxies because someone was brave enough to contemplate a donut! Oh, there's so much I want to teach you." Miss Applebaum beamed.

Almost everything Miss Applebaum said made Henry and me think differently about one thing or another. She was always sharing with us and letting us see the world through her eyes.

We went through Strawberry Fields again, heading east; basically Henry carried the briefcase and I was in charge of serving. We tried to do everything possible so Miss Applebaum could rest for a minute or two every time we came to another homeless person or family. We became a sort of roving canteen, although it was clear this was just an en route activity.

"Have you been to the museum?" Miss Applebaum asked.

"A few times," I said.

"Twice," Henry said.

On the way we saw a lot of the same things in the park we had seen the last time, but now there were a lot of Park Department trucks with dirt and fertilizer and peat moss bags. Attendants were getting the plants and trees ready for winter, using rakes and hoes and a lot of other machinery. Many more leaves had fallen, and those that still clung to the trees were bright yellow or crispy brown. Deep into the park, Miss Applebaum's breathing changed to a slight wheezing, and I looked over at Henry. We were both frightened.

Chapter Nine

The way Zelda described it, you'd think I had planned that we'd see Miss Applebaum and wait for the right moment—and then just sit her down and say, "Pardon me, Shocker, but you're going to croak." The truth of the matter was we had a duty to perform. We had to let Miss Applebaum know that her niece and the cockeyed doctor thought she was terminally ill. In the back of my mind was the simple fact that I thought Miss Applebaum should have the right to get a second opinion other than that of a quack from Weehawken. There had to be a way of being discreet about the whole matter, and I really felt it was our moral responsibility to tell Miss Applebaum. Where and when was something I didn't know, and the way it worked out, it was Zelda and I who got the shock.

At first I thought we'd tell her by the statue of the Falconer, but then an ambulance came along the roadway with its siren and lights flashing. Only emergency vehicles are allowed in the park on weekends, so the ambulance really stood out, and a lady on roller skates made the sign of the cross as the ambulance rolled by. Then I thought we'd tell Miss Applebaum near the Central Park roller coaster, but we didn't. We even passed Miss Applebaum's favorite bench, but the bulldozers and diggers had extended the trench so far and deep, even *I* had to admit it looked like one long open grave. Before I knew it, we were on the east side of the park.

Now, the east side of the park is called Fifth Avenue and that's where hordes of stuck-up and ritzy persons live. The West Side people look like peasants compared to most of the denizens of this section. The East Side buildings are cleaner. You find more expensive things in the gutters. There are penthouses with trees growing on their balconies and entire ledges are festooned with flowers and tasteful greenery. Some of the tops of the buildings have gold-leafed spirals. Everything just costs a lot more. The stores have names like Pumpkins and Monkeys. Restaurants are Chez this and Chez that. Peddlers charge more for Dove Ice Cream Bars. People wear chic clothes and walk expensive breeds of dogs. Fifth Avenue has the most mansions, many of which have been converted into fancy art palaces. The East Side has the most foreign embassies and marble facades. The neatest fruit stands. More snobby schools. Lots of high-class hospitals. And the highest paid doctors, doormen, and stretch-limo drivers. Even the bike rental shack on the east side of the park is called an emporium. As we walked by, there were a lot of tourists renting three-speeds, ten-speeds, fifteen-speeds, and all sorts of specialized equipment. One couple was even renting a bicycle built for two.

"Oh, look at them! Look!" Miss Applebaum cried out as the couple took off. "Doesn't that look like fun?"

"Yes, Miss Applebaum."

We came out of the park at East 79th Street, where one of the apartment houses across the street has a fifty-foot artistic metal birdhouse in front of it. From there, we had to walk just a few more blocks north. You could tell we were getting near the Metropolitan Museum because there were posters hawking special exhibitions such as "Ancient Art in Miniature" made possible by the Banco de Bilbao and "The Age of Sultan Suleiman the Magnificent" made possible by a cigarette company. A lot of commercial, money-grabbing companies often sponsor events like that to brainwash the public into thinking they aren't money-grabbing or selling products that the surgeon general has found dangerous to a human's health.

Finally, we reached the museum itself, which had a wall of fountains on the right and left side of it, and the main building sprawled over two blocks with eight massive Corinthian columns smack in front. There were also a lot of monstrous cement heads of antique gods and persons on the roof staring down at us. One huge flag declared that the museum was featuring a major exhibit of art called "The Hudson River School of Painting," which I never even knew existed.

We had to go up twenty-eight cement steps just to reach the front doors. Miss Applebaum was really puffing then, so Zelda and I stopped and pretended to be admiring a gaggle of Mercedeses and Rolls-Royces across the street.

"What great cars!" Zelda said.

"Two-tone mauve has always been a favorite of mine," I said.

Miss Applebaum seemed grateful for a chance to catch her breath, but she looked slightly suspicious of us, as though she saw through our pretended interest in those cars.

"Here's something more exciting," Miss Applebaum finally interrupted, gesturing to indicate the whole of the museum we were about to enter.

"Can I buy you a soda?" I asked her.

"Oh, no, thank you."

"A hot pretzel?" Zelda asked.

"Maybe some Crackerjacks or a Good Humor ice cream," I suggested.

Miss Applebaum just made believe she didn't hear us and led the way inside.

"Oh, the sights we'll see! The sights we'll see!"

For a moment she seemed wobbly like she hadn't fully recovered from the steps. Zelda and I rushed to flank her. In a moment, she recovered, but she kept checking first Zelda's face and then mine. I think she was looking for something in our eyes.

"Isn't it breathtaking?" Miss Applebaum said, looking straight up.

The museum foyer was a massive rectangle of marble with three stupendous domes high above. It was dizzying. Loads of people buzzed with excitement, and their voices echoed off the walls. They were buying tickets, checking pamphlets at the information booth, and lounging on two giant marble seating circles, the centers of which were filled with enormous live plants.

"I love to come here! I love it!" Miss Applebaum said excitedly. I think just the sight of the plants revived her, because she started breathing normally.

Zelda and I helped Miss Applebaum out of her coat, and I checked it and her briefcase in the huge cloakroom.

"What are we going to see?" I inquired.

"Whatever we're meant to see," Miss Applebaum replied.

"But what?" I said. Zelda gave me a very cranky look. I could tell from the curvature of her eyeballs, Zelda was in one of her moods where she'd give me a cranky look no matter what I said.

"It's so big, we can't see everything," I added to insert some sort of a reality factor.

"The museum will tell us," Miss Applebaum said, sounding like she knew exactly what she was doing. She headed for one of the ticket booths.

"How?" I wanted to know.

"We just go in," Miss Applebaum said. "We go in and let the museum *take* us. It's magic! It will take us through its corridors and when we get to where we should be, we'll know it. That's the only way to see any museum!"

"Oh."

I ran ahead to the ticket booth to buy the tickets, but I was getting very nervous now. And I couldn't help wonder if the museum would really let me and

Zelda know when it would be the right time and place to tell Miss Applebaum what we had to tell her.

"Oh, no, let me pay," Miss Applebaum cried out.

"No," Zelda insisted. "It's our treat."

Zelda and I had agreed way beforehand that we would pay for everything because we really didn't know how much of Miss Applebaum's money Bernice had already gotten her hands on, if any, since rumors are a lot different from facts. Whatever, Miss Applebaum looked very touched when we paid for the tickets. She checked our eyes again as though she were trying to decipher us. I had the feeling Miss Applebaum could tell whenever we weren't being completely truthful.

Anyway, I passed out little proof-of-payment buttons the cashier gave me, and we entered the exhibition area through the center hall. Immediately, on our right, was a display called "Greek and Roman Treasures," which had a lot of silver chalices, spoons, plates, forks, and other moderately interesting bric-a-brac.

"Magnificent," Miss Applebaum stated. "Oh, the ancient Greeks! There's so much to learn from them. Did you know Alexander the Great's teacher was Aristotle?"

"No," Zelda said.

"Isn't that remarkable?" Miss Applebaum said. Then she added, "Of course, Aristotle also thought that the human *heart* was the seat of intelligence."

See? That's what Miss Applebaum would do, she'd mention a fascinating fact that would make us see something from a completely different point of view.

And each time that happened, it seemed to change something very deep inside us.

We strolled onward into an area called the Blumenthal Patio that had statues of Orpheus, Zeus, Venus, and other deities with no clothes on. After that came a hallway displaying gold jewelry, wooden chairs, and religious artifacts that looked extraordinarily antique. This presentation ended in a huge shadowy room designed to re-create an old chapel. It had backlighted stained-glass windows, an alabaster rendering of the Virgin and Child, and a lot of floor-to-ceiling tapestries of subjects such as flying ladies, cherubs, and Annunciations. Miss Applebaum paused in this room. For at least five minutes she moved about, turning in slow circles like a water prospector with a divining rod. "Oh, Zelda! Henry! There are so many astounding aspects of these treasures if you look at them from a scientific point of view. When I see them, I can't help but remember the brave spirit of man."

We thought of *her* brave spirit during all this, when she felt sick and couldn't always breathe right.

She began pointing out several images of birds and animals depicted on the artifacts. "A crocodile!" she said, pointing to one carved into a triptych. "They carry their young in their mouths! And here, someone actually rendered an ancient study of the order in which humans are frightened of living things! The snake is number one! Then the spider! After that, the lion! The rat! And then the gorilla! Isn't it fascinating? And here! A long-dead Englishman carved a series of the nine words most difficult to pronounce swiftly.

See them? "Black bug's blood, black bug's blood, black bug's blood!" If you say them over and over again, the limitations of the human mouth muscles will absolutely amaze you! And can you imagine, one museum even has Charles Darwin's thirty-two fantastic pages on how worms plug their burrows! What original minds took flight to bring down such knowledge from Olympus, and preserve it for us to see!"

Miss Applebaum beamed at us. Then she turned quickly to the left and moved onward into a room filled with armor and weapons from the days of knights, serfs, and iron maidens. This exhibit was scary because there was a tableau of eight stuffed horses and knights charging right at us. I mean, they weren't moving, but they looked like they were ready to make us into shish kebabs. Everything in this room was marked with a date around 1500 and there was armor to fit men, women, children, dogs, dwarfs, corpulent rulers, and anorexic jesters. In several huge lighted glass cases were all sorts of weapons for people to kill each other with. There were spiked balls on chains, ornate pointed swords, and sharp shining arrows. I could just imagine how much blood had been spilled all over the place, or, as I say when I see a truly grotesque horror movie, "There was a lot of sauce on *that* pizza."

Miss Applebaum lingered in this room, and I was afraid she might feel this was where the museum wanted us to be today. Zelda looked completely terrified by now.

Miss Applebaum checked our faces.

"The museum doesn't want us here today," she said.

Miss Applebaum sparked suddenly, and rushed us through a huge archway into what turned out to be the beginning of the ancient Egypt area. This first room was half the size of a football field and it had the Temple of Dendur in it and a reflection pool. It was really incredible, with a slanting ceiling made completely of tinted glass. A large sign announced that the temple had originally stood in Nubia and that it had been built as the tomb for two ancient teenagers who had drowned in the Nile. The place really gave me the creeps, and I could see Zelda wasn't thrilled by it either.

"Can't you feel the vibrations?" Miss Applebaum asked. She sniffed like a bloodhound. "This is where we should be. This is where the museum wants us to be."

"Just *here*?" I asked.

"Here in ancient Egypt," she clarified. "In the Egyptian wing." She moved forward to peer into the pond, and Zelda pulled me aside.

"She's puffing again," Zelda whispered.

I didn't answer her because I was afraid our voices would echo off the temple. I just signaled her to shut up and we strolled slowly to Miss Applebaum's side.

"Should we sit down awhile?" I suggested, indicating a long, polished bench.

"No," Miss Applebaum puffed. "There's too much I have to show you, to teach you."

"Maybe we should rest first," Zelda urged.

This time, Miss Applebaum just looked at Zelda for

a second and then marched onward. "This way," she cried, picking up speed. She hung a left at the Temple of Dendur into a huge corridor filled with a lot of other old stuff from ancient Egypt. Here, it was suddenly cool and refreshing, with a lot of little machines on the walls making graph charts of the temperature and humidity. And there were sarcophagi and mummies all over the place. Also, there were huge black marble statues of scary antique Egyptian gods.

"Yes." Miss Applebaum nodded, becoming very calm. "We should be *here.*"

Zelda and I looked at each other.

I think we both knew that the moment was soon coming when we'd have to tell Miss Applebaum what we had to tell her. It just wasn't right for her not to know and not to have time to prepare. A person just shouldn't have to go through what she'd have to go through with no one to talk to about it. Nobody could ever want anyone to be that alone.

No. No one.

"Yes, the spirit of the museum wants us here today," Miss Applebaum said, her eyes shooting glances around the place like laser beams. "I have so many things to teach you. There are mysteries here! Wonders they don't even tell you about on the lighted signs or walking tours. The ancient Egyptians were the first people on earth to have bowling alleys," she exclaimed. "Isn't that extraordinary? And they trained baboons to wait on their tables! Yes, baboons! They used ketchup as medicine! And what was most fantastic is that they had no fear of death.

They were certain there was an afterlife. They were entombed with all the supplies they'd need for the next life. Everything they did before they died was a joyful preparation!"

At that very moment a chill ran through me. I felt something very frightening and very wonderful about everything Miss Applebaum had done with Zelda and me from the first day, when we brought her the begonia. With us she seemed to have begun her own "joyful preparation."

Miss Applebaum began to stroll through the exhibit pointing out one weird thing after the other.

"Oh, see these miniature boats and tiny clay people! Look at the tiny butcher shop. The teensy bakery and weaving room. The Egyptians believed these small effigies would come alive, to serve them after death. Oh, Zelda! Henry! Do you know why they call mummies mummies?"

"No," Zelda said, her voice cracking.

"No," I said softly.

"Oh, it's wonderful! *Mum!* Mum was their form of wax put over the bandages to make the body waterproof. They knew so much about death. They were exhilarated about dying. They worked out the entire brilliant process of making a mummy. First, they'd soak the body in salt water. Then they'd take out the brains through the nose! They'd remove the liver and heart with the skill of a surgeon! And they'd save the organs in beautiful clay urns that were buried along with the body. The dead were given gold for their tombs. Precious rings. Toys for dead children! Amulets! They mummified everyone! Kings! Queens!

Cats! Dogs! Even teachers! Of course, not everyone got a private pyramid." She smiled. "But there was a place for everyone, even if it was only a hole in a limestone cliff."

Miss Applebaum led us onward through a labyrinth of exhibits. She pointed left and right. She couldn't point fast enough. "Look at the mummified rats! Jars of eye paint! Sandals! Earrings! Robes! Food! Figures of their gods!"

Miss Applebaum's thoughts seemed to be coming too fast now, as though out of control. She even began to puff and then practically gasp for air as she continued to force words out of herself. Zelda and I were frightened now, especially when she turned from the exhibits and kept puffing out facts while staring right at us. We tried to interrupt her, to slow her down, but we couldn't. Suddenly, she rushed into a final exhibit room filled with tablets covered with ancient writing.

"Oh, see the hieroglyphics!" she exclaimed. "See the ancient writing of the Egyptians! The secrets of their lives and deaths that no one could understand for centuries! Do you understand what I'm saying? Do you?"

Zelda and I couldn't speak. We wanted to reach out and touch her. We wanted to find the perfect words to let her know we were hurting inside and just didn't know how to express how much we cared about her. Secrets of death were all around us, frightening, powerful, silent.

Suddenly, Miss Applebaum went silent, too.

She stared at something.

A moment later, she moved to sit on a bench in front of a huge circular stone. The giant stone was about six feet in diameter and a foot thick, and a sign said the stone was on loan from another museum. Zelda and I knew it had to be a very special stone because they had it lighted up like a monstrous diamond. And it had strange scribblings all over it. It quieted Miss Applebaum's breathing. Zelda signaled me that perhaps this was probably as good a time as any to talk to Miss Applebaum. We walked around so that we faced her this time. She kept staring at the stone.

"This is the Rosetta Stone," Miss Applebaum said. "I know now the Rosetta Stone is why we are truly here."

"Miss Applebaum," I started, "we have something we have to tell you. . . ."

She still didn't look at us.

"This stone was the key to everything," she said softly. "It is the stone that taught us to read hieroglyphics. The writings on it translated all the mysteries the Egyptians had written down for those who would come after them. For those who would live after them."

"Miss Applebaum, we need to tell you something," Zelda said, sitting next to her on the bench.

"Yes, Miss Applebaum," I said, sitting on the other side of her.

"I know, my sweet children!" Miss Applebaum smiled, looking at our faces.

"You do?" I asked in surprise.

"Yes," Miss Applebaum said. "Why do you think

we came to this room today—to this stone? You are *my* ones who will carry on what we've seen and done together, just as these mysteries were written here for others who came after." She reached one hand out and held my hand. With the other hand, she grasped one of Zelda's.

We sat for a very long time.

The three of us holding hands in front of the Rosetta Stone.

Chapter Ten

Miss Applebaum sat holding our hands for a very long time. Finally she spoke.

"Well, we must go home for tea now," she said cordially, and then released our hands.

"Yes," we said. "We must."

And I suppose this was precisely the point at which Henry and I knew things had gone so far now, there would be no turning back. Also, we both felt there would really be no one to talk to about what was happening to us with Miss Applebaum. Henry certainly wouldn't try to explain anything to his parents. And, to me, what had happened with Miss Applebaum was somehow a sort of secret trust I would not feel comfortable discussing with even my own mother and father. Things like that happen sometimes to kids. Something so private and strange happens to them that it has to be worked out without going to any grown-ups. I think it has to do with the way Nature designs kids so that they become different from their parents. Besides, I knew what was happening was something I had to explain first to myself. It was too personal and weird, and what psychologists and anthropologists might call taboo. Even my mother would have things to say about Henry and me holding hands with our teacher. She'd have very practical and compassionate things to say, but there was no way she could really understand. There were no words I could find to express my own feelings about what had happened; nor could I listen to how she felt about it. It would be only Henry and me who would truly know about this day, and the shocking events that followed.

Henry and I wanted to take Miss Applebaum home from the museum in a taxi, but she insisted on strolling back through the park. Her breathing had gotten a little better, but Henry and I stopped to admire the park at every chance we could so she could rest. We didn't get to Miss Applebaum's apartment until almost three in the afternoon. Miss Applebaum immediately started making tea in the kitchen, while Henry and I sat slightly stunned on the wicker sofa. Behind us, the Ferris wheel of plants turned slowly, lifting the dozens of gloxinias and begonias and African violets up to the last rays of sunlight.

"She knows what she has to know," I said.

"She's known all along," Henry added.

"She doesn't seem scared."

"Did you ever stop to think that maybe she *isn't* dying?" Henry asked. "Maybe that's why she's taking everything so well. She knew what we wanted to tell her, but she didn't start crying or collapse or anything."

"Maybe," I said, "she feels the way the Egyptians did. That's why she took us there today. She knew what we wanted to say."

"How can she make tea?" I wondered aloud. "Shouldn't we just leave?"

"We have to make sure everything possible is done for her," Henry said.

"What more can we do?" I wanted to know, leaning my head forward to stop a philodendron leaf from rubbing against my right ear.

"We've got to get her to the best doctor we can."

"How? Do you mind telling me *how*?"

"Time for chamomile! Time for chamomile!" Miss Applebaum wheezed, carrying in a tray loaded with a heavy ceramic teapot, cups, cream, sugar, and Oreo cookies on it. She was puffing again and looked very pale.

"You know, this Dr. Obitcheck . . ." Henry started, as I helped set up the cups on the stainless steel coffee table.

"Yes," Miss Applebaum said, "I just called him. What about him?"

"You called him?" Henry gasped.

"Yes. He's coming over now from Weehawken to give me a treatment." She noticed the expression on our faces.

"He's really a very nice man," Miss Applebaum said. She pushed aside several fern fronds and took an old black metal box out of a secretary desk. The box was about a foot long, eight inches wide, and six inches high. She placed it right in front of us. "Maybe you need *this*," she said.

"Oh," I said.

"Thank you," Henry said.

"It used to have a key, but now it doesn't lock,"

Miss Applebaum puffed. She took a cup of tea and headed out of the room.

"Where are you going?" I asked.

"I want to finish making up your exam before Dr. Obitcheck arrives," Miss Applebaum said.

"Exam?" Henry queried.

"Just a teensy one." She smiled, and then disappeared into her bedroom. We heard a typewriter start clicking away.

Henry and I sat sipping our tea and staring at the black box. Then we each nibbled on an Oreo cookie.

"What should we do with *it*?" I asked.

"Open it," Henry said.

"I don't think we should."

"Of course we should!"

Henry put the box on his lap and pressed a small worn silver button on the front of it. The top sprang open to reveal a lot of old envelopes and musty papers. Most of the contents looked like very personal documents, and I felt as though we had violated a tomb.

"Just close it back up," I suggested.

"She said we might need it," Henry reminded me. In a second he took the top half of the papers and plopped them on my lap while he started going through the bottom half.

"I don't think we should," I stressed.

"Well, I *do.*"

Henry started speed-reading his half of the papers, announcing everything he came across. "Miss Applebaum's birth certificate. Her grammar school diploma from P.S. 26. Her high school diploma from a school in the Bronx. Her New Paltz State Teacher's College diploma. Report cards. Perfect attendance awards. A photo of some old couple, probably her parents . . ."

I was horrified as Henry even started reading some of the personal letters, but he insisted I shut up and examine my half. My pile had her NYC Board of Education teaching license, photos—complete with captions written on the backs—of Miss Applebaum when she was a naked baby on a fluffy rug and when she was five years old riding a pony. There were photos of her with what looked like all sorts of relatives—her grandparents, and gray-haired people who appeared to be from Europe. There was a picture of a shaggy collie, a handsome man in a police uniform, and Miss Applebaum as a young lady in a raccoon coat. There were letters from her mother and father. Her parents' death certificates and canceled checks for perpetual care of their graves. Some old relative's naturalization papers. These were memories of a lifetime! They came pouring out of the box and all over the sofa. Precious bits and pieces of Miss Applebaum's life were everywhere. The things she cherished. Things to remember. There were legal papers and obituary clippings. There was so much of Miss Applebaum that we had never even thought about. Much more than her being just our teacher from school. What was most amazing was that it all came as a surprise to us. We hadn't known much about her. There were dozens of letters from former students, letters that seemed so personal I couldn't open them. But Henry did. He skimmed them a mile a minute, quoting phrases from them like, "How can I ever thank you . . ." and "You were the best teacher I ever had . . ." and "Thank you for the recommendation . . ." and "I don't know what I would have done without you. . . ." There were special letters from grateful kids who had gone on to the Air Force or work or college or marriage, and all sorts of different adventures. So many of Miss Applebaum's former students had taken the time to remember her. They had written about their gratitude to her and their loving memories of her. "Remember when I wanted to run away and you took me out for a pizza?" one student wrote. Sometimes a single phrase was like the tip of a traumatic iceberg, and we could just imagine the whole story that lay hidden beneath it.

"Thank you for lending me the money for my graduation corsage."

"You really taught me that I was worth something."

"You were always there for me during my parents' divorce."

"I'll never forget that you found me my first job."

"You were so wonderful."

"I think of you often."

"Remember when I wanted to run away."

"Remember when I was so lonely."

"Remember when I wanted to kill myself."

Henry finished going through his half and reached over and took the rest of my pile.

"They really loved The Shocker," Henry said.

"Yes," I agreed, as I opened a flat Leatherette

folder. I glanced through the papers inside. They appeared to be newer and very important. It took me a moment, but I finally realized I was looking at Miss Applebaum's health plan and her medical insurance I.D. cards. One booklet was actually a reference directory of all the doctors in Manhattan covered by her insurance.

"Henry, look," I said, giving them to him. He had barely skimmed the materials before we heard Miss Applebaum coming back down the hall. Henry kept the Leatherette folder, but we quickly put everything else back into the black box.

"Quiz time!" Miss Applebaum puffed, as she came into the room. "Quiz time!"

She seemed very jolly, except for her breathing problem, and she passed us each a sheet of paper. From what I could see, Henry got the original exam sheet from the typewriter, and I had a carbon copy.

"No fair peeking," Miss Applebaum said.

She made a place for me to sit on an upholstered stool near the model of a flower blossom and told Henry he could stay on the sofa. Then she handed out pencils and told us to do our best.

"Begin *now*!"

"Yes, Miss Applebaum," we said, just like we were back in her classroom.

"You'll have fifteen minutes, so you can really think about each question," she said generously.

I stared at the words on my paper.

It was one of the most challenging, succinct examinations Henry and I had ever been given, even by Miss Applebaum's standards. Henry says I shouldn't

MISS APPLEBAUM'S QUIZ

NAME____ DATE________________

_____ 1. How wide is the Statue of Liberty's mouth?

a) 10 feet b) 20 feet c) 3 feet d) 80 feet

_____ 2. How many chemicals are in cigarette smoke?

a) 3 b) 23 c) 200 d) 900

_____ 3. How long a tunnel can a mole dig in one night?

a) 10 feet b) 20 feet c) 70 feet d) 300 feet

_____ 4. How fast can a sneeze travel?

a) 10 mph b) 60 mph c) 100 mph d) 600 mph

_____ 5. How many drops of water are in a teaspoon?

a) 50 b) 120 c) 500 d) 1000

_____ 6. Members of Louis XIV's Court used to bathe in:

a) wine b) oil c) mud d) crushed strawberries

_____ 7) Women used to tie this onto the ends of their beds to stop themselves from becoming witches during the night:

a) holly branches b) mistletoe c) onions d) garlic

_____ 8) The major export of Lichtenstein is:

a) tulips b) beer c) chocolate d) false teeth

_____ 9. Leonardo da Vinci invented an alarm clock that woke the sleeper by:

a) speaking to him b) waving at him c) laughing at him d) rubbing his feet

____ 10. Whatever its size or thickness, no piece of paper can be folded in half more than:

a) 4 times b) 7 times c) 12 times d) 40 times

write the answers here, because someone might want to take the test, so he's putting the answers in his next chapter. Besides, I don't want to write about what happened when Dr. Obitcheck arrived. It was so terrifying!

Chapter Eleven

Zelda and I weren't even halfway through the quiz when Dr. Obitcheck arrived. Miss Applebaum answered the door wearing the same blue terrycloth bathrobe she had worn the first day when we visited her, and she was puffing about the same. She let the doctor in.

"You know Henry and Zelda," Miss Applebaum said.

"Yes," Dr. Obitcheck grunted, clutching his Jack the Ripper satchel. He was dressed in another wrinkled pin-striped suit, and his eyes were as weird as ever. Maybe it was just the way the late afternoon sun bounced off the plants and antique lab equipment, but his right eye looked like it was staring at the ceiling and his left eye appeared focused on the floor.

"Hello," we said.

"I'm just giving my young friends a quiz," Miss Applebaum explained. "Do the best you can." She waved at us, and then disappeared with him down the hall to her bedroom. Zelda and I squirmed like greased eels because we knew very well the doctor would be sticking Miss Applebaum with that humongous hypo. We also figured that draining the fluids away from Miss Applebaum's lungs would help her breathe, but I suddenly thought she deserved much better than that. Maybe he wasn't a good doctor! Maybe she didn't have to die. Maybe someone else could help her more. I filled in the rest of the quiz as quickly as I could. I began to study the Directory of Participating Physicians and Other Providers booklet that was in the Leatherette folder. Upon perusal, it turned out to be a directory because it told what all the fancy specialization names for doctors mean right in the front. It had headings like cardiology, dermatology, podiatry, hematology, and at least twenty other specialties. It even listed Dr. Obitcheck in Weehawken, and he was billed as only a general practitioner. I could tell from the definitions that the kind of doctor Miss Applebaum really needed would be an "oncologist," and I was relieved to see Miss Applebaum's health plan included four such doctors in Manhattan. If they were in the book, then that would mean the health plan would pay for them. The Freudian Octopus and the Cockaloony Bird would often discuss scintillating health plans over dinner, so I knew a little about them. There was a complicated explanation on the first page of the directory that said this health plan would pay for everything except five dollars for each office visit and that it would pick up eighty percent of any other bills beyond a three hundred dollar deductible. What fascinated me most was that Miss Applebaum had given us the black box at all. I mean, Zelda and I knew she was old because of the way she acted, but every time she did something a little senile or wacky, there was a lot of sense to it. Even Zelda remarked that when Miss Applebaum gave us the box, she was symbolically putting herself in our hands. It's a very scary feeling when an adult does that to kids. Zelda and I began to feel more and more that Miss Applebaum not only needed our help, but that she was asking us for it in the only way she knew how. I know it was Zelda and I who chose to visit Miss Applebaum in the first place, but the thought crossed my mind that perhaps we had all chosen each other a very long time ago. Miss Applebaum for her reasons. Zelda and I for our reasons. After all, it was Miss Applebaum who let us earn service credits in the lab at school. She had hired us. She had trusted us. And all the extra experiments she taught us how to do were far and above the call of duty. Maybe she had picked us out then. Drafted us, so to speak. Zelda would say that Miss Applebaum could have bonded with us subconsciously, and that we were drawn to Miss Applebaum for our own subconscious needs. It even crossed my mind that maybe the freaky force drawing us all together in a very bizarre and weird way was connected somehow to death. Whatever, Zelda and I had barely decided what we had to do, when we heard Miss Applebaum laughing in her bedroom. Then, there came the sounds of her and the doctor returning through the hall. When Miss Applebaum and Dr. Obitcheck reached the front hallway, I was still holding the Leatherette folder. Miss Applebaum stared right at me and the folder and then inquired without puffing at all, "Have you both finished your quiz?"

"Yes," Zelda said. "It was very interesting."

"Provocative," I added.

"I have to get back to Jersey," Dr. Obitcheck said grouchily, his eyes flitting all over the place.

"Oh, please join us all for some yogurt," Miss Applebaum requested, joyously collecting our test papers.

"I really can't," the doctor said.

"But you *have* to," Miss Applebaum insisted. "I'm sure my young friends have some matters they'd like to discuss with you," she added, the shock practically sending me into a cactus.

"No, we don't," Zelda said, her eyes on red alert.

"Of course you do." Miss Applebaum smiled. She took the doctor by the arm and led him through the living room into the jungle at the L bend. "And I haven't shown any of you my book collection," she bubbled.

"I only have a minute," Dr. Obitcheck said, disentangling himself from Miss Applebaum. Zelda and I stood up and joined the safari.

"I know it's hard to see the books, but behind practically every plant is a bookcase." Miss Applebaum motioned, pulling an orange tree aside.

Indeed, all the walls here were lined with the thickest bookcases I'd ever seen.

"That's very nice," Dr. Obitcheck said with a touch of uncalled-for sarcasm.

"They're special bookcases. I had them built so

they can hold books *three* deep," Miss Applebaum said proudly. "Look! Aren't they wonderful. Aren't books extraordinary?" she added, running her fingers over shelves of bindings. She had all sorts and sizes of books with titles like *Great American Scientists*, *The Beauty of Plankton*, *The Mystery of Man*, *Cosmic Phenomena*, *Heaven on Earth*, and *The Beauty of Life.* There were books by authors such as Lewis Carroll, Colette, H. G. Wells, Margaret Mead, and hundreds of other ordinary famous people, too. "Oh, and just look! You pull one book out, and there's another right behind it. I rotate them like my flowers on the Ferris wheel. Without brilliant books like these, I could never have created such a quiz," Miss Applebaum declared. "In fact, without them, I could never have even lived!"

"I have to go." Dr. Obitcheck harrumphed and turned to leave.

"We need a second opinion," I suddenly blurted out at him.

"I beg your pardon?"

"Miss Applebaum needs a second opinion about her condition," Zelda amplified.

"My, this gardenia bush is dry," Miss Applebaum said, turning her back on the doctor. Suddenly, she seemed very busy with her plants and paid no attention to us. It was as though she had to shut us out and pretend what was being said was *not* being said.

"It wouldn't change anything," Dr. Obitcheck said, glaring in two new directions at once.

"Well, we think it might," I said.

"Ah, the gloxinias are going to bloom again! Such trumpets!" Miss Applebaum said to a row of pots.

Dr. Obitcheck said to me and Zelda, "I wish it would help, but it won't."

He now shot his words at Miss Applebaum.

"Miss Applebaum, I discussed this with your niece, and we agreed."

"As long as I've grown ficus trees, I've never fully understood precisely how much water they require." Miss Applebaum smiled, completely ignoring him. "They're so temperamental."

Dr. Obitcheck stared now with one eye twitching between Zelda and me and his second eye frozen on Miss Applebaum. Miss Applebaum still paid no attention to him and began dusting the leaves of a giant elephant ear plant.

Dr. Obitcheck looked intensely insulted, as if we had violently defiled the American Medical Association or something.

"You do as you like," he said very unkindly, and then marched toward the door with his eyeballs completely spastic. In a moment he was gone, slamming the door behind him.

Miss Applebaum sat down and started grading our quiz.

"I'll bet you did just fine," Miss Applebaum said, beaming. Actually, we didn't do very well, because the correct answers were: 1) c 2) d 3) d 4) c 5) b 6) d 7) a 8) d 9) d 10)b. But I guess the important thing was that Miss Applebaum now seemed very, very happy. Maybe even *hopeful* was the word for it. It was Miss Applebaum who suggested we play Goonie and Elevator Roulette, and before we knew it, it was dinnertime. Zelda and I treated Miss Applebaum to a pizza with extra cheese and large Diet Cokes delivered from Ray's Original, and I must say the entire evening became quite a lovely party. Zelda and I didn't get home until after ten P.M.

Monday morning, Zelda and I went to school, but we spent the whole lunch period checking the Directory of Participating Physicians and Other Providers. Three of the four doctors listed as oncologists had the same address on Fifth Avenue, and we were very surprised and pleased to see that Miss Applebaum's health plan let any subscriber go to such a fancy address. We picked one of the three, a woman doctor by the name of Harriet Silver, and figured if Miss Applebaum didn't like *her*, we could check out the other two. Besides, with all their offices on Fifth Avenue, that meant their building faced Central Park, and we knew Miss Applebaum would really like that. The directory even listed the hospitals the doctors were associated with, and Dr. Harriet Silver worked out of Parkview Hospital, which also was on Fifth Avenue and was right next to Mt. Sinai Hospital, which everyone knows is one of the best hospitals in the world. We knew sight unseen that Dr. Silver would know a lot more about up-to-the-minute cures and medicine than anyone could possibly know from Weehawken, New Jersey. Above all, we thought if we got Miss Applebaum to a top doctor, she'd at least have a chance. That's what we wanted to do, give her the best chance!

By the end of the school day, I had set up an appointment for the next morning at eleven, and called Miss Applebaum. I told her what we'd done.

"I can't wait to see you," was all Miss Applebaum said on the phone. "I can't wait!"

By nine A.M., Zelda and I had called in to school to make certain we wouldn't get any cut cards, and then we met Miss Applebaum in front of her building at ten A.M. sharp. We wanted to take her across the park by cab, but she insisted on walking, and this time, she had her briefcase filled with stacks of peanut butter and jelly sandwiches and Ziploc bags of Velveeta cheese cubes. She was dressed neat as a pin in one of her tweed jobs and gave the first sandwich to Helen's hand under the newspapers at 72nd Street. Then we gave sandwiches to practically every other homeless person we passed. To be truthful, some of the homeless persons looked just like plain freaked-out derelicts to me, but Zelda always gets cranky if I call them that. Anyway, we made it over to Fifth Avenue and walked up past the Metropolitan Museum all the way to 96th Street. Our conversation was mainly about things like ducks migrating and the miraculous effects of mulch on rhododendrons, but Miss Applebaum acted more like we were going on a picnic than anything else. She was so cheerful and optimistic and scintillating. She really seemed to be our own loving, energetic, and perfect grandmother, which is what I had told Dr. Harriet Silver's receptionist she was when I had made the appointment.

Dr. Silver's office turned out to be on the northeast corner of Fifth Avenue and 96th Street, and her location was even more beautiful than I had imagined. Furthermore, her office was part of a medical arts complex, and the whole complex was physically connected to Parkview Hospital itself, which meant you didn't even have to go outside if it was raining to get from the medical arts complex to the hospital. We didn't find out all that until later, but the three of us were very enthusiastic the moment we entered Dr. Silver's waiting room. It was so bright and airy and had the best magazines I've ever seen in any doctor's or dentist's emporium.

"We're here for Miss Applebaum's eleven o'clock appointment," I told the cheerful receptionist. "We called yesterday."

"Oh, yes, we're expecting her," the receptionist said, giving a big "hello" to all of us.

"Hello," Miss Applebaum said.

Zelda and I mumbled "hi," but we were both overwhelmed and impressed by all the beautiful furniture in the waiting room. It had a fantastic blue rug lit by focused track lighting, and it was so ritzy and state-of-the-art that we didn't know where we would sit first.

"You can give me the health plan I.D. card, and fill out this form," the receptionist said, handing us a piece of paper on a clipboard. "The doctor will be with you shortly."

I gave over the I.D. card, while Zelda took the "personal information" form. We finally decided to sit on a plush leather sofa and chair combo, which was in one corner near the window. Zelda filled in all the information she knew about Miss Applebaum, and Miss Applebaum did all the rest, such as writing her social security number and checking a long list of boxes concerning her personal and family health history. By the time we had done all that and thumbed through the cartoons in a *New Yorker* magazine, Dr. Harriet Silver herself came out. She looked like a mature, distinguished, and graying Madame Curie, wearing a white jacket, and her hair was swept up in an impressively professional manner. Then, after the introductions were over, Dr. Silver told Miss Applebaum that she was very lucky to have two such fine and thoughtful grandchildren, but that she'd have to borrow our "Grandma Alice" a while for an examination. I had forgotten to tell Miss Applebaum about our little grandmother prevarication, but Miss Applebaum understood immediately.

"They're the finest children any granny could have," Miss Applebaum said.

Everything was extraordinarily friendly and perfect, so Zelda and I were feeling full of hope when we let Miss Applebaum go with Dr. Silver. Maybe she wouldn't die! The last we saw of the two of them they were heading into an examination room, and Miss Applebaum was chatting about snake plants. We knew we had done the right thing and there was nothing for us to do but to wait and keep our fingers crossed. Zelda even hummed as she checked out a copy of *Vogue*, and I was pleasantly surprised to find an edition of the *Global Gazette* under a *Wall Street Journal.* The *Gazette* had to have been left by some more earthy patient, because it was in complete contrast to the high caliber of the rest of the reading materials. The headline stories were "WOMAN GIVES BIRTH WHILE WATERSKIING," "NUDE PIN-UP GIRL EXPOSED AS A MAN," and "SPACE ALIEN CURED MY ACNE, SAYS HAPPY TEEN." Not only did I have a chance to read those articles, but I also perused other reports about a plumber's head that got stuck in a toilet overnight, and the easiest way to lose one's tummy in a week. Zelda not only finished *Vogue*, she got through a *Fortune* and three *Psychology Todays*.

A few other patients arrived during the course of all our reading, although they weren't there to see Harriet Silver. As it turned out, George Kreb and Harry Loeb, the two other doctors listed in Miss Applebaum's health plan, shared the waiting room, but they each had their own receptionists. And all the other patients looked very wealthy and refined, but you could tell they were sick. One man was missing patches of his hair, and a lady patient wore dark textured stockings that looked like they had designs in them, but when we looked closer, we could see she had a lot of strange marks all over her skin.

It was past noon when something unusual happened, and somehow we knew it had to do with Miss Applebaum. A male orderly in a white coat entered the waiting room from a pair of swinging doors off to one side, and he was pushing an empty wheelchair. He disappeared into Dr. Silver's examination room, and in less than five minutes he came out again pushing Miss Applebaum in the wheelchair. Dr. Silver was right behind them, and she ran interference as we rushed toward Miss Applebaum.

"We have to admit your grandmother to the hospital," Dr. Silver said.

"Are you all right, Grandma?" I asked Miss Applebaum, because I didn't want them doing anything to her against her will.

"I'm fine," Miss Applebaum said.

"Are you sure?" Zelda asked.

"Yes, my darlings"—Miss Applebaum beamed—"yes."

Before we knew what was happening, the orderly picked up speed and pushed Miss Applebaum through the swinging doors like she was going into a strange and eerie funhouse. It all happened so fast, we didn't have much time to think.

"We have to run a lot of tests," Dr. Silver explained. "Your grandmother really needs to be hospitalized."

"Is there a chance you can do something?" I asked straight out.

"There's always a chance," Dr. Silver said.

"That's what we want," I said.

"When can we see her?" Zelda wanted to know.

"She needs X rays, a blood work-up, and a complete physical. It'd be better if you went home and . . ."

"When can we see her?" I repeated Zelda's question, staring straight into Dr. Silver's eyes.

Dr. Silver looked a little wary, like I might bop her on the head if she didn't answer me.

"You can check with admissions at Parkview Hospital and they'll tell you what room she'll be in. Your grandma's a very lovely lady," Dr. Silver added, and headed back toward her office.

"WHEN CAN WE SEE HER?" I called out again so loudly that the woman with the textured stockings dropped her *Good Housekeeping.*

"Check with admissions," was all Dr. Silver echoed, and then she disappeared into the corridor.

Zelda and I stood like idiots in the middle of the waiting room. We really didn't know what to do. Everything seemed okay, but it felt strange to have walked in with Miss Applebaum and then see her rolled out.

"Quick, let's *go!*" I said to Zelda.

I grabbed her hand and pulled her toward the swinging doors.

"You can't go that way!" the receptionist called out. "You have to walk around to the hospital. . . ."

Before anyone could stop us, we were running down a ramp that led underground into a mind-boggling network of passages connecting the medical arts building to Parkview Hospital. It was impossible to tell which of the passageways the orderly had taken Miss Applebaum down. Let me say now that the sights Zelda and I saw underground were quite something. They made *Alice in Wonderland* look like a lark. It was a whole bizarre world down there, with nurses and doctors and orderlies pushing patients on gurneys and all sorts of wheeled gadgets. We saw a lot of deliverymen and kitchen workers and storage rooms with doors ajar. One oil deliveryman was walking right in front of us, and he had

"TANKS ALOT" embroidered in big letters on the back of his overalls. There was a sign that said "TO ALL BUILDINGS AND PAVILIONS," so we followed that passageway until we came to another one with blue, red, and yellow along the walls. I figured this was a color code to get people from one place to another, but I didn't understand it at first. A very old lady the size of a leprechaun was wheeled by, wearing eyeglasses with very thick lenses. She looked very sick. All the trash cans in the passageways had signs with freaky faces that said "PITCH IN," and at every bend there was a large convex lens hanging from the ceiling so people rushing from one place to another could see what was coming to avoid a crash. Across from a department marked "RADIOLOGY" was a huge cafeteria the size of a football field. It smelled like they were cooking kangaroo burgers and horsemeat stew, and its decor was even more depressing than the one at Andrew Jackson High. We finally found a sign that showed what all the stripes meant. It indicated where places like CASHIER, C T SCAN, EMERGENCY, KLINEBERG PAVILION, PHARMACY, REHABILITATION, AMBULATORY SURGERY, and all sorts of other places were. Zelda and I decided to follow the light-blue stripe because it was supposed to be the MAIN CORRIDOR. We figured that had to take us eventually to something that would look like the main lobby of the hospital, and from there we could find out what room Miss Applebaum would end up in.

"We'll find her," I said.

"It's a very fine hospital," Zelda said, wanting to believe it.

"It really is," I agreed.

I guess we both knew deep down that it was just plain common sense that Miss Applebaum had to be examined. We stopped to catch our breath at a bulletin board that had a picture of one of the hospital workers called Phyllis Mook. "Phyllis Mook, nursing," a notice said. "Phyllis has proved to be an excellent role model for new employees. She readily and generously offers assistance, and ably and efficiently carries out her duties." And it was signed by her supervisor. Zelda remarked that it was really a very nice way to provide employee incentive by having a Worker of the Week exhibit, and Phyllis Mook did look very pleasant.

After about another ten minutes of peeking in and out of all sorts of departments filled with laboratory equipment, we found the main lobby by taking an elevator up one flight. The GIFT SHOP, regular WAITING ROOM, "RELATIVES OF SURGICAL PATIENTS" WAITING ROOM, and the ADMISSIONS OFFICE were right there. This area was extremely clean and modern, and I had to admire that straight off. It even had IN-HOUSE PHONES like they have in deluxe four-star hotels, and I picked up one phone marked INFORMATION. In less than five seconds, a melodious lady's voice came on and asked how she could help. I asked her if she knew what room Alice Applebaum would be in, and she said 19D right off the bat, but she also added that visiting hours were only between six and eight P.M. I thanked her very much and then immediately pulled Zelda into an elevator and pressed 19. I had no intention of waiting until six P.M. and thought we'd probably find Miss Applebaum in the room putting on some kind of white gown the hospital would give her for the tests. I really didn't know what to expect, but I was glad no doctors or official-looking persons got into the elevator and tried to stop us.

Everything was fantastically luxurious in the elevator. Shiny brass. Red rug. Even the emergency phone compartment was artistic. It felt like we were going up in the Sherry Netherland Hotel. And when the door opened on the nineteenth floor, we were really pleased. Zelda and I stepped out into one of the most tasteful hallways we'd ever seen. The air smelled like delicate flowers, and there was expensive art all over the place. Original oil paintings and numbered prints lined the walls, and there were sculptures practically every twenty-five feet with special modern works under glass. It didn't look like a hospital. It had an extremely chic waiting room just for the nineteenth-floor visitors. And even the room directory itself was unobtrusively wrought, providing clear directions to 19D. There were a few fashionably attired patients strolling about like they were in a private garden, and we didn't see a gruesome sight anywhere. Of course, the hallway was about a block long and a few nurses could be seen going from room to room in the distance. As it turned out, Room 19D was right near an exquisite nurses' station, but nobody stopped us from going into the room. Naturally,

I'll have to admit I waited until all the nurses were looking in a different direction because I always think it's better to be safe than sorry. I didn't want them to enforce the visiting hours now that we were so close.

Zelda and I literally gasped when we saw the inside of 19D.

It was splendiferous.

It was fantastic.

It looked like a heavenly place to take a rest. Everything was so spectacular that the last thing we noticed was the bed. The first thing that took our breath away was a huge picture window of Central Park. We rushed to the wall of glass and knew that Miss Applebaum would be joyous when she saw it. You could see the whole Central Park reservoir, and to the south were all the wonderful spots Miss Applebaum had shown us. We could even see half of the toy boat pond and Miss Applebaum's favorite bench on the knoll. Of course, it was very small in the distance, but it was there nevertheless. The window made our spirits feel like we could just fly out over the park and above any problems there could possibly be in the world. The room was unbelievably large, and shaped like a gargantuan thick cheese wedge. It was a suite! It had one door leading to a private spacious bathroom that looked like it was out of *House & Garden.* There was even a separate alcove with a very impressive spotless petite kitchen including its own microwave oven. The bed was as soft and white as a goose, and it had a dazzling matching chrome side table and bedstand. The wallpaper was a sky blue and the rug was so plush, it felt like feathers.

I closed the room door just enough so if one of the nurses passed by, they wouldn't throw us out, then checked the color TV and all the control switches including one that made the fabulous bed move into all sorts of positions and heights. We were filled with hope. And everything we wanted for Miss Applebaum was there. There wasn't a chance anyone could die in a room like this. It took us over twenty minutes to check out everything, and when Miss Applebaum hadn't arrived by then, I just called downstairs on the streamlined color-coordinated phone.

"It usually takes at least two hours for a new patient to finish the entrance examination," the operator kindly informed me. Her voice sounded so vibrant and caring, she made it sound like Miss Applebaum was being admitted to a country club.

"Two hours," I told Zelda.

"What'll we do?" Zelda wanted to know.

"Go shopping!" I said.

I knew Zelda got the idea, because she beat me out of the room, and in a flash we were in the wondrous elevator heading back down to the main lobby. I might as well tell you right now that the security at Parkview Hospital was zilch. We walked right by doctors and nurses, and the only security guard was on the first floor. Not a single person asked us what we were doing. I suppose if we were trying to leave with an IBM typewriter or a thousand-pound Xerox machine, they might say something, but I could see we'd have no trouble coming and going. Actually, all we did was go out the Fifth Avenue exit and around the corner to Madison Avenue, which is the section where we always read that Jackie Kennedy Onassis and other philanthropists go shopping. Zelda and I wanted to buy a few things for Miss Applebaum's room so it'd be even more delicious and appealing than it was. I had almost forty dollars and Zelda had taken out a hundred dollars from her savings account. My parents were giving me twenty a week for the "course" I was taking, and Zelda still had a few hundred left in the bank from when she worked in the Metropolitan Opera's children's chorus. The kids in the chorus got paid only ten dollars for each rehearsal and performance, but Zelda was in three televised versions of operas, which paid three hundred and fifteen dollars each. Whatever, we both were prepared to spend every penny we had if it would help Miss Applebaum.

The first thing we noticed about Madison Avenue on the block right behind the hospital was that there was an excessive number of florists and pharmacies. I had never stopped to think that such stores would be natural in any hospital district because everybody buys flowers and toiletries for sick people. It took us almost an hour to shop, but the items we bought for Miss Applebaum were: 1) a bowl of germinating narcissus bulbs, also called "white pepper," from the Bloomin' Fine florist; 2) a jar of Vitabath, three lilac soaps, and a bottle of Maja perfume from Jerome's Drugstore; 3) a box of chocolate fudge, one bag of pistachio nuts, and a selection of Côte d'Or Candies from The Chocolatier; 4) a banana cake from

Sarabeth's Kitchen; 5) a marble cheesecake from Miss Grimble's; and 6) a Jackson Hole hamburger to go, in case Miss Applebaum was hungry. We also got ourselves each a hamburger, but ate it on the Jackson Hole premises. Then we bought a few more items we thought Miss Applebaum would get a kick out of, including a deck of cards from Penny Whistle Toys, a copy of *Eat Your Way to Health* from The Book Nook, and a moisturizer from the Dorchester Dermatology Shop, which had a big sign in its window that said it offered "a new wrinkle in quality skin care." We just wanted to make certain Miss Applebaum would have a few snacks and basic necessities to get her started, and then we'd get her whatever she really wanted. We had all the shops gift wrap everything so it was very festive, and we ended up getting an entire fruit basket from Tom's Thai Fruit Market. We had so much stuff, we could hardly walk back to the hospital. There we just marched right by the security guard on the first floor, who was so busy talking to a pulchritudinous candy striper that he didn't even see us. We could have been carrying in a bazooka and he wouldn't have known it. It's no wonder you always read about hospitals getting ripped off. Any personnel that did see us just smiled and admired our armfuls of great gifts.

We made it into the same beautiful elevator as before and went straight up to 19D. The room was empty again and just as striking as before. In a way we were glad we got back before Miss Applebaum, because it gave us the chance to arrange the flowers, fruit, and presents so that the room looked extraordinarily tempting. We moved the position of the white peppers and fruit basket about a dozen times before we felt we had everything in the perfect position. And I'd be lying if I didn't admit Zelda and I each sampled a Côte d'Or chocolate while we waited. But that's what we did. We waited and waited and Miss Applebaum didn't show up. However, a nurse did.

"What are you doing here?" the nurse asked. She didn't sound nasty. Only curious.

"We're waiting for Miss Applebaum," I said.

"I don't understand," the nurse said.

"This is Miss Applebaum's room. She's a new patient."

"There must be some mistake," the nurse said. "This room is reserved for Mrs. Remington."

Zelda and I didn't quite know what to say, but the nurse picked up the phone and called downstairs. As it turned out, whoever was on patient information had made a mistake by telling us Miss Applebaum was going to be in 19D. Either that or we had heard wrong.

"Alice Applebaum is in *Nine* D," the nurse clarified. "I'm sorry," she said, sounding like she really meant it.

Like she really, *really* meant it.

Zelda and I were sorry, too. All we could do was gather up all the gifts and get back in the elevator. We thought 9D might be just as nice a room, and maybe it would even have a better view of the park. Miss Applebaum might even like being on a lower floor, because then she could see the faces better on children and everybody else in the park. But I suppose we knew that wasn't going to be the case the moment we stepped out of the elevator onto the ninth floor. There was no art on the walls on the ninth floor. There were no sculptures and no luxurious lounging area. What there was were *wards*. We followed a big black arrow that indicated which way to turn for 9D and moved slowly down the corridor. Zelda and I could hardly bear to look in each ward as we passed them. What I remember most was glimpsing oxygen tanks and ordinary sinks and old sick people. The nurses and orderlies were scurrying back and forth and none of them sounded mellifluous.

Finally we stood at the door to 9D, which was also a ward.

There were eight beds. Four on the left and four on the right. Half of the patients in the room looked like they didn't have very long to live at all.

Then we saw Miss Applebaum.

She had a bed by a window. It wasn't a picture window. It was a small, ordinary window that looked out onto an air shaft and a wall of soot-covered bricks. There was no park. There was no sun. There was nothing beautiful.

We walked slowly toward Miss Applebaum carrying our offerings, which now seemed painfully out of place. Miss Applebaum saw us coming. She was sitting up in bed, wearing a stark white hospital gown, and there was a small bandage on the left side of her neck.

"They cut me," she said to us. "They cut me."

Then, our beloved teacher burst into tears.

It was then we knew we should just have let things be the way they were. What we had done was not going to help at all.

Chapter Twelve

Henry and I didn't know what to do or say. We stood silent next to Miss Applebaum's bed until she finished crying.

Finally, Henry said, "We'll get you out of here."

Miss Applebaum stopped crying. She dried her eyes with a tissue from a plain brown dispenser on her bedstand.

"I have to stay," Miss Applebaum said simply, looking directly into our eyes. For the first time, it seemed Miss Applebaum was completely in reality. "Maybe this will help me," she said.

"You need a better room," Henry said, and then spun on his heels.

"We'll be right back," I assured Miss Applebaum and ran after Henry. I caught up with him just as he reached the nurses' station. He started yelling. "Miss Applebaum needs a room like they have on the 19th floor. Why did you cut her? What are you doing to her? She's not staying here!" Henry just kept bombarding the nurses with one angry statement after the other. What was strange was none of the nurses looked like they were disturbed about being attacked. In fact, neither did any of the aides and orderlies look surprised at the way Henry was behaving. It was like they had seen the scene hundreds of times before and knew the best way to handle someone with Henry's anguish was to let him get it all out. By the time he had gotten everything off his chest, a young man in a white jacket and with a stethoscope around his neck eased into position in front of Henry and me and told us his name was Dr. Markham. Dr. Markham looked like he was barely out of college. He was short and thin, but sounded extremely concerned and intelligent. He told us he was the physician in charge of the ninth floor and that he understood how we felt. What he did was use psychology on us, but in the best sense of the word. In fact, he sat down with us on a row of chairs near the elevators and told us things we needed to know about Parkview Hospital. He let us know in the nicest way he could that the kinds of rooms like 19D were so expensive they required not only health plan benefit payments, but deposits up to twenty thousand before anyone was even admitted to them. He assured us that the Admissions Office had gone over with Miss Applebaum all the choices she had, and that she herself must have approved of her room and type of treatment. The more he talked, the more Henry and I realized he was just doing his job. Everyone at the hospital seemed to be doing their jobs. It was only that Henry and I wanted so much more for Miss Applebaum. We had hoped for so much! Dr. Markham ended up being very helpful and told us our concern for our grandmother was understandable, and Henry and I were finally convinced the medical care Miss Applebaum would be getting was going to be of very high quality. There simply would be no frills.

We went back to Miss Applebaum's bedside. We felt much better with the initial shock gone, and even Miss Applebaum now looked comfortable and hopeful. We helped her unwrap the gifts. And the whole ward seemed to be not as frightening. Most of the beds still had female patients in them who looked like they were terminal, but somehow, after we managed to focus in on their faces, they seemed to be very nice and very brave human beings. Miss Applebaum immediately asked us to pass out her chocolates to everyone. The other patients said things to Henry and me like "Thank you," and "What lovely hair you have, young lady," and "I have a grandson just like you, young man." They actually spoke like normal people regardless of what they were going through. Dr. Markham even took time to stop by Miss Applebaum and explain why they had taken a biopsy of one of the glands on her neck. He didn't promise any instant cures about anything, but he very carefully explained that it was necessary to examine tissue samples from Miss Applebaum in order to decide on precisely the right treatment. Then all sorts of people began to show up. A nicely dressed old lady volunteer came by with a cart of free candy bars and cupcakes to pass out. And an old man volunteer pushed another cart with books and newspapers that the patients could check out or buy if they wanted. By four o'clock, a lot of candy striper high school girls showed up to puff up pillows and say hello to the patients, and before we knew it, the dinner carts loaded with trays of food arrived. I knew it would be time for Henry and me to leave.

"We'll see you tomorrow," I said to Miss Applebaum.

"Make sure you go to school," she said.

"We'll see you *after* school," Henry promised.

Miss Applebaum leaned forward, reaching one hand out to us. Finally, she found the words she wanted to say. "Would you bring me some things from my apartment. Would you mind?" Miss Applebaum asked. Then, she handed me an envelope. "I made a list of things and where they are. And would you mind watering the plants? Please water my plants!"

"Of course," I said.

"We'll take good care of everything," Henry promised, examining the contents of the envelope. Besides the list of notions and things, it contained Miss Applebaum's keys and her Chase Manhattan automatic teller card.

"I've written down the bank card code for you," Miss Applebaum said. "You just put the card into the machine, press the code numbers, and the machine will give you three hundred dollars maximum per day. Take out all you can every day. We're going to need it. We'll need it very much," she pleaded.

"We can't take your money," I said.

"Take it for me. I'll want you to use it," Miss Applebaum urged. "I want Helen to have coffee and donuts. I want all my friends in the park to have as much as you can give them. Roast beef sandwiches.

Salamis. Bagels with lox. Milk! Please give them as much as you can before Bernice finds out. *Please.* She'd use the money her own way."

Bernice.

We had forgotten about Bernice.

Now, it isn't necessary to know everything that happened during the next forty-six days that Miss Applebaum was in ward 9D. A few general facts will reveal all that has to be known.

Henry and I said we would tell everything important, so we have to record the very terrible fact that at the end of forty-six days, Miss Applebaum didn't have many hours left to live. The first week, Henry and I went crazy running around Parkview Hospital and barging into Dr. Silver's office practically every day. The reason we couldn't express any of our real sorrow to Dr. Markham and the nurses on the ninth floor was because Dr. Markham had been transferred soon after to another floor. In fact, *all* the nurses, except for one tough head nurse called Miss Ruth Perez, were transferred every week. It became clear the entire ninth floor of Parkview Hospital was devoted to terminal patients, and that the ordeal of having to work with them was so upsetting that the hospital made it a policy that none of the workers be exposed to such sadness for more than a week at a time. What outraged Henry and me was that there was no continuity except for Miss Perez. Practically every time Henry and I had established a rapport with a nurse or doctor and felt confident that Miss Applebaum was getting the best treatment possible, that nurse or doctor would be transferred. And Dr.

Silver made it clear from even the second day she was simply going to monitor Miss Applebaum's progress, which she did about once a week. Even with her fancy address, she soon didn't pretend there was any hope. She didn't believe very much in miracles. We wanted to take Miss Applebaum home then, but Dr. Silver said they would keep her more comfortable there. The biggest fight Henry and I had with the staff during this whole time was when we heard Miss Perez being rude to the patients. She'd say things like "Stop bellyaching" or "I told you, I'll give you the shot at five P.M., and that's when you'll get it!" or "If you don't like your dinner, don't eat it." We thought she was the cruelest person on earth, and we decided to tell her off. Henry got her out by the nurses' station one night and called her everything in the book, but sturdy Miss Perez didn't blink an eye. What she did was let Henry finish bellowing, and then she pulled us aside and spoke very gently to us. "The patients need someone like me to fight with or they give up their will to live," she let us know. "If you give in to their every wish, they lose their life force. Life is a *struggle*, and I have to provide a bit of that struggle. I have to play the bad cop," she said sadly, vulnerably. And she actually made sense to some degree. I think that was the only time Miss Perez let us see through her tough act, and even if we didn't completely agree with it, we had to admit she wasn't as terrible as we had first thought.

Another fact Henry and I had overlooked was that Miss Applebaum wasn't suddenly dying in the space of forty-six days. Her niece had filed Miss Applebaum's retirement papers for her in the spring, which meant that Miss Applebaum had been sick for over six months. By the time we had even brought her the begonia plant, she was far into her illness, but we didn't realize how far. All we knew now was every day when we went to see her, she was continuously losing weight and her breathing was becoming increasingly difficult, regardless of how much fluid they removed from her chest. I've repressed almost everything that happened during the whole forty-six days except for three events. At least for me, it was three events. The first event was when Henry and I first went to Miss Applebaum's apartment and let ourselves in with the key. The second event was a dream I had. And the third event was a horrible encounter with Bernice. I think I can only tell about my dream, which I had in the middle of the night on November 3rd.

My Dream

There is a stage with a blood-red curtain, and the curtain lifts to begin a play. I see two very sad children walking through a black, cold forest. One is a boy with armor locked over his heart, and the other is a frightened girl with a single long braid. The children are lost and terrified of the forest. They walk by giant shadowy trees and dark, undulating ferns as white vapors of a fog drift through the forest. Slowly, it is no longer a play in a theater but a very real event that is happening. There are other frightened people in the forest, and like the children they are all looking for a way to escape. The children begin to cry, and walk on alone. They come out of the mist and see a strange old lady sitting on a chair. The lady seems happy, and she's dressed like a wizard. This lady wizard is feeding hundreds of fantastic, huge ravens. The lady holds a large basket brimming with bread, and she breaks pieces of the bread into crumbs that she throws into the air so they fall like snow. The birds feast, as the old woman turns and sees the sad children. She waves to them, slowly, smiling. She calls to them, and the children go to her. They sit with her around a lawn table. The children know that the old woman is magical. They know she is a good witch. And the girl tells the lady that she has found a great treasure and would like to take them all away. She wants to treat them all to a magnificent journey, and buy them everything they've ever wanted. She wants to take the lady with them onto an airplane and bring them to grand and distant lands. She tells the old lady that she'd like to take them on the glorious excursion of a lifetime. The boy answers first, smiling at the little girl. He tells the girl that he would very much love to go with her. He thinks that he deserves such a trip because he's been a wonderful friend to the girl. He would love to fly with her anywhere and travel as far as she would like to go. He would like to see the Seven Wonders of the World, and royal palaces in India, and the great shining rivers of the universe. But the lady wizard doesn't speak. After some time, the girl again invites the old woman. She asks the woman over and over again if she'll come with them on this fantastic voyage. Finally, the woman does answer. She says that she can't go. The little girl still asks her why not? Why can't she go? And this time as she asks, the great ravens surround the lady's chair. Still, the woman smiles.

"Please come," the girl begged.
"I can't," the old woman repeated.
"But why? Why can't you come?"
"Because I am dead."

Chapter Thirteen

I don't blame Zelda for having to skip around a little in recording the events that happened. As long as I'm able to fill in the gaps, we'll manage to get all the truth down. It'll just be a little rearranged according to what our brains will let us talk about.

It was almost dark the first night Zelda and I left Miss Applebaum at the hospital, so we took a cab.

"Chase Manhattan, on the corner of 64th and Broadway," I ordered the driver, who looked like one of those New York taxi drivers who have a metal plate in their heads.

"We're going home!" Zelda said, practically punching me in the arm.

"No, we're not!"

I insisted on getting to the bank right away to see if Miss Applebaum's automatic teller card really worked. It wasn't that I wanted to get my hands on any of her loot for myself, but Miss Applebaum said she didn't want Bernice to get it.

"It's our duty," I told Zelda.

"It is not."

"It is *so.*"

We got out of the cab right in front of the bank. By

this time the main offices of the bank were closed, but with an automatic teller card you can stick it into a slot and it opens a door that lets you into the front lobby, where the money machines are. Naturally, you have to look both ways to make certain muggers don't rush the door while you're going inside and put a gun to your head to help influence your financial transactions. But Zelda and I made it just fine, and when I put Miss Applebaum's card into the machine, I was able to press a button to check the balance in her savings account. Zelda almost fainted when she saw Miss Applebaum had over ninety thousand eight hundred dollars. No wonder Bernice didn't want us around. Right off the bat, I knew we could take out three hundred a day for a lot of days, although I didn't know precisely what Miss Applebaum wanted us to do with so much money. To get the three hundred that night, I had to punch in the code number first and then the dollar amount, and a sign came up on the screen that asked me to lift open a metal drawer below it and remove my cash. You could actually hear the machine counting out the bills, and it was a very stimulating sound. I took the money, the machine printed out a receipt and a message saying, "THANK YOU FOR USING CHASE MANHATTAN. PLEASE REMOVE YOUR CARD." It was really a very competent and courteous machine.

"What are you going to do with Miss Applebaum's money?" Zelda insisted on knowing.

"Leave for Brazil," I told her.

She didn't like my little joke. Actually, what we did was go straight over to Miss Applebaum's apartment.

Zelda wanted to get all the things Miss Applebaum needed that she had written down. What they were were two nightgowns, her Py-co-pay toothbrush, Colgate toothpaste, slippers, Listerine, her pair of reading glasses, a yellow legal-size pad, a Piggyback pen, her Max Factor lipstick, an eyebrow pencil, Evening in Paris perfume, Chanel dusting powder, and a few other items that would be the envy of any participant in a scavenger hunt. Anyway, Zelda had her work cut out for her, and she wasn't particularly happy about going up again in the creaking elevator.

"I feel very funny about this," Zelda said when we got out on the eighth floor.

"I knew you'd say that," I said.

The keys Miss Applebaum gave us worked fine, and in no time Zelda and I were inside Miss Applebaum's apartment. I'd be lying if I didn't say that it was extraordinarily spooky. Zelda ran around putting on all the lights she could find, and she certainly found a lot of them. The apartment went from looking like a mausoleum at midnight to something like the Amazon at noon. Zelda even put on the lights to the Ferris wheel and it started turning. It was as though the apartment and plants had all come completely alive. I saw plants and trees and scientific equipment I hadn't even noticed before.

"I'll pack Miss Applebaum's things," Zelda said.

"I'll hide the money," I said.

"Where?"

"Someplace no one would look!" I went straight to the ex–Andrew Jackson High human skeleton hanging on its stand behind the sofa. Even though its skull was cracked and it didn't have all its ribs, its jawbone hinge worked perfectly. I opened its mouth and put the money smack up inside the skull. It made a rather foreboding piggybank, I thought.

"That's disgusting," Zelda said.

"It's utilitarian," I said.

Zelda just looked at me like she was going to gag and made for Miss Applebaum's bedroom. I stayed in the living room checking out a few ficus trees and Miss Applebaum's collection of magnets for a while, and then decided to look through some of the closets. The hall closet was sort of regular with functional ladies' coats and practical wool hats, and an umbrella that had a stylish wooden duck's head for a handle. And the closet down the hall near the bathroom had only clean white sheets, dull towels, lots of bars of Dove soap, and a bottle of Head & Shoulders. On the whole, the closets' contents looked very traditional, not that I was expecting to find gold bullion or wolf-bane or black candles or anything like that. Those two closets just looked like a nice old lady lived in the apartment. I got bored fairly quickly and began to check out the area of the living room just beyond the L bend where most of the bookshelves were. Even with all the lights blazing, I could hardly see the walls because of all the trees, but I did spy a closet door that was practically overgrown by ivy. The long vines had grown down from huge hanging baskets of moss, and I wasn't even going to open that closet. Then I thought, Why not? Actually, it was the only spot where I *did* feel a little strange prying open the door. It was like I was violating a pharaoh's tomb, and King

Tut might pop out to bop me on the head. I actually had to break some of the vine creepers that pressed against the door like very thin, ghoulish fingers. By moving a couple of large palms, I was finally able to get the door open.

As the light flooded in, I was quite shocked at what I saw. The closet was completely filled with *men's* clothing. I don't mean like attire from last season's Barney's sales. I mean men's clothing like you might see in a World War II museum. There were Navy sailor shirts and uniforms that looked like they were from the 1940s. There were polka-dot bow ties and a flashy tuxedo with huge lapels and about ten pairs of antique shoes that were everything from flashy two-tone black and white to powder blue. There was even a raccoon coat like you sometimes see people wear in Laurel and Hardy films. I couldn't resist putting the coat right on and barging straight into Miss Applebaum's bedroom to show Zelda.

"Look at this, will you?"

Zelda screamed. "I thought you were a bear!"

She was standing in front of a huge bedroom closet with its sliding doors wide open. Right off the bat, I could see about ten dresses the Andrews Sisters would have been proud to wear for U.S.O. shows to entertain the troops. Zelda pulled out one dress that had silver sequins and crocheted beading all over it and was trimmed with peacock feathers. Actually, a lot of the clothes in both Miss Applebaum's closet and the closet I'd found looked like things nostalgic rock 'n' roll stars would give their eyeteeth for when they wanted to look unique. Both of the closets had so much style, we almost fainted. We started running back and forth between the rooms checking out everything in those two closets. Zelda found a second raccoon coat in the bedroom closet that looked like it matched the one in the man's closet.

I had an uncontrollable urge to grab one of the pillows off the bed and throw it at Zelda, catching her completely off guard.

"You idiot!" she laughed.

In a flash she picked up the pillow and came running at me, but I grabbed a second pillow from Miss Applebaum's bed and we started smacking each other as hard as we could with the pillows. I was the first one to get really tired, so I just plopped on Miss Applebaum's bed and let Zelda bang me with the pillow about fifty times. We had never laughed so hard in all our lives. Finally, Zelda was exhausted, too, and she dropped laughing to the floor on the other side of the bed. We were puffing like steam locomotives and were really whacked out. I couldn't even lift my head off the bed to see Zelda on the rug. Eventually, I saw her hand creep up like a tarantula on the other side of the bed, and finally she pulled herself up and lay down next to me. We were still laughing when we noticed something on the bed where the pillows had been. It was a photograph. An old and faded photograph. It had to be something Miss Applebaum cherished and had kept under her pillow for years. It was a picture of a young girl and a sailor kissing in the front car of a Coney Island roller coaster. We could see plain as day that the girl was Miss Applebaum when she was about twenty years old. And the sailor boy looked like he really adored her. And the photograph itself was set in a little cardboard frame that said, "Alice and Steven forever." It was strange, but up until that moment we had never even imagined that at one time Miss Applebaum had been young and lovely, and dated boys, and did crazy things like ride in the front car of a roller coaster. And she kissed. She was once a pretty, sweet girl who kissed a handsome sailor, and they were in love. Alice and Steven forever!

Then we thought of Miss Applebaum now.

Miss Applebaum in the hospital.

For a long while, we lay on Miss Applebaum's bed holding on to each other.

Chapter Fourteen

Zelda still isn't feeling up to writing yet, so I'll have to continue. I don't blame her, because I guess this is the hardest part to tell about. Zelda was able to give you a few highlights of the routines at Parkview Hospital, but there was a lot more going on while we were learning about those. Most of the time Miss Applebaum had us running around like chickens with our heads cut off. On school days Zelda and I would usually get up very early and deliver treats to Miss Applebaum's charity recipients before we went to school. When we didn't do it in the morning, we did it right after school. Miss Applebaum went to the trouble of making up a list for us so we'd know everyone she wanted remembered. Zelda and I simply called it Miss Applebaum's list.

Miss Applebaum's complete list included at least thirty stops. Zelda and I found it took us a half hour just to shop for the things at the deli down the block from the Dakota. We knew Miss Applebaum gave out food, but we didn't know she had a specific route she took and knew almost every homeless person in her section of the park. She told us there was another woman by the name of Naomi Larson who gave out

MISS APPLEBAUM'S LIST

HOMELESS PERSONS	LOCATION	FAVORITE TREAT
Helen	West 72nd Street entrance	Coffee and glazed donuts
Mr. & Mrs. Mollari	Strawberry Fields, behind big rock	Two bagels with cream cheese
Joe	In cardboard box behind the Falconer statue	Liverwurst on rye
The Dutton family	Under bridge near carousel	2 coffees for mother and father ½ gallon of milk for their kids
Rocco and Jimmy	Behind Shakespeare	2 Twinkies
Rose, Hannah, and Emily	Behind Einstein	Box of giant Oreos
Fiddler on the Hoof	Toy boat pond	Put dollar in violin case

free food on the southernmost section of the park around the ice-skating rink and children's zoo, and that a very nice elderly couple called Mom and Pop O'Malley had a route up near "no man's land" and the park reservoir. Zelda and I found Miss Applebaum's route extremely exhausting until we figured out who and where everybody was, but even then it took a good hour walking at a good clip and pushing a borrowed supermarket basket. Also, it was getting cold, so a few of the homeless went south, we were told, to parks in Florida and New Mexico, and some days one or two of them would be missing because the police had them picked up and put in a nuthouse.

All this was going on while Zelda and I kept up our schoolwork, studied for tests, and managed to get over to see Miss Applebaum for at least an hour every evening. I also kept up the withdrawal of three hundred dollars a day until the skull of the skeleton had loot bulging out of its eyeballs. Of course, Miss Applebaum kept increasing her food gifts the closer it got to the holidays. From November 20th on, she added entire quarts of eggnog, loaves of seven-grain bread, and pounds of Dutch Pal cold cuts. One day, she wanted everyone to have a can of Campbell's tomato soup and a box of matches. Miss Applebaum kept running things right from her bed no matter how thin or weak she was getting. It seemed every week the doctors ordered some new test done to her or tube attached to her. It started with an intravenous tube that was supposed to make certain Miss Applebaum had enough water in her system to make it possible for her to get chemicals and radiation treatment. Some days, we'd arrive to see her and they'd have her down in the laboratory for another biopsy or X ray. But Zelda and I and Miss Applebaum stayed as hopeful as we could for as long as we could. We played Goonie. Monopoly. Trivial Pursuit. Scrabble. And Miss Applebaum loved helping us with our homework.

"Be original!" she kept telling us.

"That's too old hat! Think of something new!"

"Try making a diorama to prove an algebra equation!"

She'd give us hints on how to do our assignments so that they were startling. Refreshing, she'd say. I had to write a composition for history on the American judicial system, and Miss Applebaum suggested

I write it from the point of view of a horse that was found guilty of sorcery in New Jersey and hanged. She gave Zelda a unique way of discussing economics by taking off from the fact that multibillionaire oil tycoon John Paul Getty had a pay phone in his mansion. That was the fantastic thing about Miss Applebaum. She knew much more than science. Her knowledge spread into every field of study and endeavor. Even when the chemotherapy she was getting started to make her hair fall out, she still pressed forward making Zelda and me reach for the unique and inventive. Sometimes, we'd arrive at her bedside just as they had added a new drip bag of chemicals to her intravenous, and she wouldn't have enough strength to lift her head from the pillow. Even then, she'd just close her eyes and tell us things like "If you got rid of all the space in the atoms that go to make up a camel, you *could* pass the camel through the eye of a needle." She'd whisper, "Three fourths of all species of mammals are rodents." She'd tell us, "The eye of a giant squid is larger than a person's head." Sometimes, we'd think she was asleep, but then her lips would move and she'd say something fantastically stimulating like "On the average, each human being contains two molecules of Julius Caesar's last breath." It just seemed as though she could never stop teaching us.

I don't think I can put off any longer telling you about our showdown with Bernice, so I'll get it over with right now, and then Zelda will probably be able to write the next chapter. It wasn't that we didn't think about Bernice. We must have thought about her at least once a day from that first night when Miss Applebaum, Zelda, and I were playing Elevator Roulette doing the cancan, and Bernice appeared. It's very hard to forget anyone with a hatchet face and a chilling disciplinarian voice. I suppose we were meant only to meet Bernice at elevators, because that's exactly the way it worked out at the hospital. We had told Miss Applebaum to write to Bernice so she'd know where she was, and tell Bernice that she had decided to get treatment at Parkview Hospital. We knew Bernice would be showing up sooner or later, and we also knew it wouldn't be a barrel of laughs if we happened to run into her. What we didn't know was that she'd be waiting for us smack in front of the elevators on the ninth floor of the hospital at seven o'clock in the evening. Zelda was holding a bag of Miss Applebaum's favorite treat, which was Pick Up Sticks Restaurant's shrimp in lobster sauce and pork fried rice, and I was holding a supply of egg drop soup and fortune cookies. We had been chatting sedately while riding up in the elevator about how happy Miss Applebaum would be to see the food, even though she couldn't eat very much anymore. We were really looking forward to seeing her.

Then the door opened and we saw Bernice with her buzz-saw face and fancy dyed blond Connecticut-matron hair. This night, she looked like Nessie the Loch Ness Monster itself.

"I've been waiting for you," she said, as though she were going to rip our throats out.

"Hello," we said, stepping off the elevator holding our bags of Chinese food.

"Are you satisfied now? Are you?" Bernice started to immediately scream at us. Her voice was so loud, everyone at the nurses' station turned and several orderlies and nurse's aides came out of the wards.

"Miss Applebaum's getting the treatment she needs," I said quietly, stepping to shield Zelda in case Bernice did try to haul off and punch us.

"There is no treatment for her!" Bernice roared. "There never was!"

"It's not too late," I said.

"It was *always* too late!" Bernice bellowed. "You had to tell her she was dying! You had to give her hope! Well, don't you see what you've done!"

"We've given her more of a chance," Zelda said.

"She could have been spared this!" Bernice literally screamed. "She could have lived her last days in peace. You've let them cut her! You've let them experiment on her! You've murdered her, you stupid, hateful children!"

"We're not stupid and we're not hateful!" I automatically yelled right back at her. At that moment I couldn't sensibly process every remark she had hurled at us, but I could see Bernice was in as much pain as we were about Miss Applebaum. There simply seemed to be a lot more than dollar signs in her eyes.

"Then *you* stay with her. *You* watch her suffer. You're a couple of sons of bitches, that's what you are," Bernice hissed at us. She got into the elevator.

"You want her to die in this hellhole, well then, you've got it, you killers!" Bernice burst into tears. We were shocked, and for the first time we felt Bernice actually loved and cared about Miss Applebaum. The elevator door closed and she was gone. Zelda and I were left standing there holding the Chinese food with everyone looking at us. Without saying a word to Zelda, I knew she was thinking and feeling exactly the same as me. It had just never really entered our minds that Bernice could have been acting out of love all along. Everything was just so complex. We had just wanted to think the worst about Bernice because that was the only way we could have any hope. We couldn't be horrible kids just because we wanted hope. We just couldn't be.

Zelda and I started walking slowly to ward 9D. And we felt so bad that there was nothing to prepare us for what was waiting for us. Miss Applebaum was in the last bed on the right, as usual. Her window still looked out onto the brick air shaft. We were so stunned by our encounter with Miss Applebaum's niece that we didn't notice the change in Miss Applebaum until we reached the foot of her bed. In addition to her intravenous hook-up, they now had two tubes coming down over her head and attached to her nostrils. The other ends of the tubes led to an oxygen tank. Miss Applebaum looked awful.

Miss Applebaum tried to smile.

"We've got shrimp and lobster sauce," Zelda said.

"And fortune cookies," I added. I knew it sounded stupid, but I couldn't be blamed for any words that came out of my mouth. And when Miss Applebaum spoke, all she said was, "Please buy me a small plastic fan? One that runs on batteries. Please?" It was such a strange thing to ask for.

"A small fan, please . . ."

We looked at Miss Applebaum. She looked at us. I think that was the moment all three of us knew it would soon be over.

Chapter Fifteen

I can't put all the responsibility on Henry to write about Miss Applebaum's last days, although there aren't too many more details about Miss Applebaum's stay at the hospital anyone has to know. Henry and I did buy Miss Applebaum the small plastic fan she wanted, but she never really used it. By her forty-fifth day at the hospital, they stopped her chemotherapy and Miss Applebaum refused to take any more of the pills intended to help keep her heart going. The evening of that forty-fifth day, Henry and I arrived at Miss Applebaum's bedside, and she simply said, "Please take me home."

It took us until the next morning, which was a Saturday, before we could rent a wheelchair from Delancy's Hospital Supplies on West 81st Street, and bring over winter clothes, including Miss Applebaum's mouton lamb coat, and blankets. Miss Applebaum insisted that we shouldn't hire an ambulance or orderly or even a visiting nurse. Head nurse Ruth Perez, Dr. Harriet Silver, and the doctor of the week for the ninth floor, Dr. Manley, all tried to talk Miss Applebaum out of leaving, but she told them there were a lot of loving friends waiting for her at her apartment and that she wanted to be with them. By 11:15 A.M., Miss Applebaum was in the wheelchair and signed out of Parkview Hospital, and Henry and I and Nurse Perez brought her down to the lobby. The one rule the hospital insisted upon so that no one could sue them was that the patient had to be escorted by a staff nurse to the lobby before being entrusted to anyone else's care. Henry gave Nurse Perez a ten-dollar tip, we all said good-bye, and Henry pushed Miss Applebaum out to Fifth Avenue while I carried the overnight bag packed with her nightgowns and notions.

"We'd better take a cab," Henry said.

"No, please," Miss Applebaum said. "Please take me home through the park."

Henry and I looked at each other and really didn't know what to do. In the cold December light of day, we had to admit the Miss Applebaum we were taking home from the hospital was very different physically than the one we had brought to the hospital. Even wrapped in her coat and blankets, she looked too sick to be out. Some of the people on the street stared at her as we went by. Miss Applebaum lifted a corner of one blanket to partly hide her face.

"Through the park, please," she repeated.

"Yes," Henry said.

To get into the park, we had to push Miss Applebaum a little ways down Fifth Avenue past the Metropolitan Museum. As we went by the museum entrance, the gargoyle faces of ancient gods looked like they really were staring down at us, and I remembered our visit. Miss Applebaum, Henry, and

I walking through the galleries of life and death in ancient Egypt. The Rosetta Stone. Huge flags in front of the museum snapped like whips, and the water still gushed from the front fountains.

Once we were past the museum, the wind hurtled against us as it rushed out of the cement canyons to the east. But here, the sun was shining bright against our faces, and the sky itself was a startling winter blue. At the entrance to the park, a solitary old man was trying to sell hot pretzels and chestnuts, cans of Sunkist orange soda, and Mott's apple juice. But the sidewalks were deserted.

We turned in to Central Park at a point where the sidewalk sloped steeply downhill. Henry had to hold back the wheelchair or it and Miss Applebaum would have picked up tremendous speed. The most obvious change in the park since we had last strolled through with Miss Applebaum was that the trees had lost all their leaves. Only an occasional evergreen stood out like a lost Christmas tree. We walked by a huge stone slab that was supposed to be a work of art by a man called Randolph Gans. At least, he had the good sense to call it "Unidentified Object," which is what it looked like. There were posters announcing upcoming activities in the park such as the "Belvedere Castle Family Workshop: Making Holiday Cards" and "The Dairy Children's Class" about "Shiny Shapes and Bright Balloons." Soon, all about us the branches of the huge trees looked like monstrous bony fingers reaching over us for the sky. Dead leaves were underfoot and so moist and crushed that they looked like they had been already well transformed into earth. The smell of near winter dilated the nostrils, and despite the barrenness and complete death of the leaves, the fragrance was strangely exhilarating. The park now looked like vast English moors, rolling land lying naked for the wind to play. The black lampposts stood out like burned stakes from the ground. Construction and playground repairs were going on in the park with a haste, because more than anyone, the workers knew a deep freeze couldn't be far off. Masonry workers repaired an overpass. Cobblestones were being replaced along a path. Park crews rushed to get the last of snow fences into place before it would be too late. All deeds that needed to be finished while the earth was still moist and soft were being done. Mothers pushed their babies in strollers. A scant few children played about the statue of Alice in Wonderland. We reached the toy boat pond. Henry and I were shocked.

"They've drained the pond."

"Yes," Miss Applebaum said.

Dead leaves and mud were all that was left of the pond. Gone were the young and old weekend sailors with their remote controls. No miniature tugboat or submarine. A huge flock of sea gulls and wild ducks had gathered in the center, where a few small puddles lay. The birds were excited, picking over the last of any trapped small fish and crayfish who hadn't the good sense to dig deep into the mud for the winter.

"Take me to my bench," Miss Applebaum said.

We pushed Miss Applebaum up the knoll to her favorite spot. From here, all Henry and I could see was without magic. The cafe was closed. There was no violin to be heard. No carousel calliope in the distance. Tractors and bulldozers were moving earth. The pipeline had been laid down like a huge dark artery, and its open trench still split the hillside like a wound. The beauty of the spot was gone for Henry and me. All was desolate. Depressing. The entire area behind Miss Applebaum's bench was still being ravaged by men with shovels. A cement mixer was noisily forming a new curb in the distance. Henry turned Miss Applebaum's wheelchair so she could see whatever she wanted to see. Henry and I looked at each other. Miss Applebaum glanced up and caught our painful exchange.

"Don't be sad," she smiled. "Winter has a purpose, too."

She looked at the long trench and seemingly endless stretch of black pipe that lay at its bottom.

"Take me home now," she said, cheerfully. "There's so much to do."

Chapter Sixteen

Zelda took the keys and opened the downstairs door of Miss Applebaum's building. I gently pushed the wheelchair with Miss Applebaum into the lobby. What was really weird was that Zelda looked like she was ready to cry and I was scared stiff, but Miss Applebaum seemed to be in the best mood I'd seen her in since we had last played Elevator Roulette! In spite of her fragile appearance and our knowledge that she was close to death now, Miss Applebaum actually made perfect sense. She told us exactly what to do. We got her into the elevator and up to the eighth floor, and the second we rolled her into her apartment she started singing, "Hello, plants! Hello, plants!" She didn't belt it like Tina Turner or anyone like that, but she was very focused and clear. She couldn't have weighed more than eighty pounds by now, but she acted like she was going to a party. She had me start the flower Ferris wheel and asked me to roll her around to a couple of dozen of the larger pots while she checked their moisture. "You really have to be especially careful with ficuses," she said. "You and Zelda have done a wonderful job! Wonderful!"

Zelda went straight into the bedroom to turn down Miss Applebaum's bed, and when I rolled in Miss Applebaum, it was very easy to lift her into her bed. Miss Applebaum looked completely exhausted, but very, very happy. All along she was having trouble breathing, yet it didn't seem to interfere with her joy at being back in her home. She just kept looking around the room and nodding happily to all the plants and furniture.

"We should order a hospital bed," I said.

"Oh, no," Miss Applebaum said.

"They rent nice ones with air mattresses and all types of equipment like they have at the hospital," Zelda said. "Delancy's said they would even send over oxygen and whatever you needed."

Miss Applebaum smiled. "I won't need anything," she said.

Miss Applebaum lay with her head against a big white pillow. She looked like a baby bird that had fallen out of its nest. We wanted to do everything we could, but we didn't know how to help her now. She looked at Zelda and me. I thought I saw sorrow in her face. I didn't get the impression she was sad about anything that was happening to her. I think for that moment she was feeling sorry for *us*.

"Would you please get paper and pen?" Miss Applebaum requested. "In my desk," she added. "In the desk."

"Of course," I said.

"Would you like something to eat or drink?" Zelda wanted to know.

"No, thank you," Miss Applebaum said.

"Maybe yogurt?"

"No."

I found a pad and a pen and scooted back to the foot of Miss Applebaum's bed.

"Pull chairs over," Miss Applebaum requested.

Zelda found a small swivel chair and sat at Miss Applebaum's left side, and I moved a wicker chair so I was sitting at the right side of the bed.

Miss Applebaum spoke slowly, almost in a whisper. "I'm going to be leaving," she said.

Zelda and I didn't know what to say. Zelda looked at the floor and I found myself mumbling and turning a Papermate ballpoint pen over and over in my hand. "There's over ten thousand dollars left in the skull," I said. I was really babbling nonsequiturs. I hadn't even told Miss Applebaum I was keeping her money in the skeleton, so I mumbled some more and told her now. "There's over ten thousand dollars left in the skull."

"A very good bank," Miss Applebaum smiled. Then she took a full minute to catch her breath, and continued. "You and Zelda use the money to keep my friends until spring. Would you do that? Keep Helen and all the others alive?"

"Yes," I said.

"Yes," Zelda said.

"Just keep them until spring. It will be warm then and they'll find someone else to help them. I know that. Just don't let Bernice take it. She's a nice girl but too much of a pragmatist. And tomorrow, call the cockroach lady."

I thought I was hearing things.

"What cockroach lady?"

"Call the museum. Tell them you want to talk to the cockroach lady. She works in one of the turrets. She's a naturalist . . . very old . . . and she works there studying cockroaches and centipedes. She's very famous. They write articles about her. She loves living things. Just ask for the cockroach lady. I don't remember her name. I can't remember now. . . ."

"We'll call her," I said, jotting down the words, "cockroach lady."

"She'll know who should have my plants. Tell her about the plants. . . . They need to be picked up. They need a new home. Probably the botanical garden. She'll probably say that—the botanical garden. They'll come. Take the plants. But give one of the little plants on the Ferris wheel to each of the apartments in this building. Just leave one in front of each door. No note. There are a lot of caring people in the building. They'll love a plant. Did you make a note of what I said?" Miss Applebaum asked.

"Yes," I said, scribbling away at a mile a minute.

"The cockroach lady will also tell you who should get the scientific apparatus."

"Won't the museum want it?" Zelda asked.

"The city museums don't have much space left," Miss Applebaum said. "Boston University. Or a museum in Philadelphia. They send students in vans. Call them. But ask the cockroach lady first. . . ."

"We will," Zelda said.

"And *you*," Miss Applebaum said, lifting a finger to point first at Zelda, and then at me. "You both take a favorite plant. They like you. You are children who love living things. You take some of them and the magnets and some things to remember me. Take something you like. Take what you like. . . ."

"May I have the skeleton?" I asked, and then I wanted to yank my tongue out. "I don't mean the money. I don't have to take the skeleton." I drifted. "I could still hide the money in it, of course, but I don't need the skeleton, I could take the wind tunnel. . . ."

"Please take them." Miss Applebaum smiled. She slowly turned her head to look at Zelda. "What would you like?"

Zelda couldn't answer. She began to speak and her voice cracked. Finally she was able to say, "May I have the model of the flower?"

"Yes," Miss Applebaum said. "Yes. That would be perfect." She started to cough.

Zelda hurried to the kitchen for a glass of water. I pulled tissues out of a Kleenex box. Zelda rushed back practically spilling the water on Miss Applebaum, but Miss Applebaum didn't seem to notice. I wasn't sure she could even recognize what a tissue was anymore. Finally, Miss Applebaum stopped coughing. Zelda patted her lips dry.

"I think we should call a doctor," Zelda said softly to her.

"No," Miss Applebaum said. "Get the typewriter. . . ."

"The what?" we asked.

Miss Applebaum started pointing toward a large potted bush. "My . . . Smith-Corona . . . typewriter . . ." she clarified.

I got up and had to go straight over to the bush before I could see a small white table against the wall with an extremely old typewriter on it. It looked like something you'd see in a silent movie. Miss Applebaum told me to bring it over. I picked up the whole table, typewriter and all. I remember feeling very queasy because I was certain Miss Applebaum was going to make us type up her last will and testament.

"That's right . . . bring it here," she said. "Put a piece of paper in it. . . ."

I put the typewriter smack in front of Zelda.

"You want me to type?" Zelda asked.

"Yes," Miss Applebaum said.

"Type *what*?" I asked.

"A letter . . ."

"To who?"

"To *Bernice*," Miss Applebaum wheezed. Just the mention of her niece's name again was enough to summon up the knot of guilt that lay ever-present in our stomachs since the evening when Bernice yelled at us at the hospital. Even so, we really had no idea of what Miss Applebaum would want to tell her at this point.

Miss Applebaum began speaking.

Zelda began typing.

The words came slowly. When it was finished, Miss Applebaum's letter really shocked us.

Miss Applebaum signed the letter using the Papermate pen and had me leave it on her nightstand. "Bernice will find it . . . sometime . . ." Miss Applebaum said.

DECEMBER 12

DEAR BERNICE,

I AM LEAVING TO SAIL AROUND THE WORLD. MY HEALTH IS MUCH IMPROVED. I FOUND AN OIL TANKER THAT WILL BE STOPPING IN MANY SOUTH AMERICAN AND ASIAN PORTS. THE TANKER ONLY ACCOMMODATES A FEW TOURISTS. IT IS SOMETHING I'VE ALWAYS WANTED TO DO. I DON'T KNOW WHEN I'LL BE BACK. I SEND YOU MUCH LOVE. I MAY DECIDE TO STAY IN VENEZUELA.

ALL THE BEST TO YOU AND YOURS,

Alice

"Yes," we agreed, but I didn't know what we were agreeing to. Miss Applebaum closed her eyes. She began to move her fingers, as though she were counting in a dream. It turned out she was resting before she would make a final request of us. Her eyes opened. Now every motion of her body became diminished. Her fingers moved slower. I wished Miss Applebaum would have died at that very moment. If Zelda and I had to be with her for the very end, I wanted it to be like sleeping. If death was merely going to sleep, I felt Zelda and I would be able to live without our own fear of it. Death as sleep. It would be okay. But it wasn't to end that way.

No lies.

Not now.

Miss Applebaum opened her eyes wide. Her lips began to move. Zelda and I moved closer to hear. Miss Applebaum wasn't trying to speak. She was trembling. We moved to sit on the bed. Miss Applebaum could look up now and see us both without turning her head.

"I'm *frightened*," Miss Applebaum said.

We couldn't speak. We didn't know what to say. We didn't want it to end like this. Our smart and brave Miss Applebaum saying she was afraid. I didn't think we could answer her, but I found myself saying, "You don't have to be afraid, Miss Applebaum."

"No," Zelda echoed.

"You've been a wonderful person," I said.

"You've been kind to everyone," Zelda said.

We now each held one of Miss Applebaum's small hands.

"You've lived bravely."

"You've helped so many."

"You've been a great human being. . . ."

Then we went silent.

We looked into her eyes. Miss Applebaum's lips no longer trembled. She spoke for the last time.

"Bury me in the park," she said.

We heard the words, but couldn't dare to believe them. We leaned closer.

"Bury me in the park," she repeated, and slowly closed her eyes.

She was dead.

Miss Applebaum was dead.

Chapter Seventeen

Henry and I did everything we could. We tried calling for help. We called Dr. Obitcheck. He was angry about the call, told us to call whatever fancy doctor we had dragged her to. Dr. Harriet Silver only had an answering service. We did reach Dr. Manley on the ninth floor of Parkview Hospital. He told us how to test for Miss Applebaum's pulse. There was none. He told us to hold a mirror to her mouth and look for water vapor. There was none. He told us we shouldn't have taken her home. He reminded us he had warned us that she didn't have long to live. We called Bernice and got a recording saying, "We can't come to the phone just now, but please leave a message." We didn't. We ended up doing nothing. There was nothing we could do to make us feel less guilty.

Almost nothing.

We sat next to Miss Applebaum until late that night. Henry didn't have to call his parents, but I called my mother and told her Henry and I were going to a late movie and that she shouldn't worry about me.

"Zeldaaaaaaaa!" she said.

"Really, Mom," I said.

It took Henry and me a long time to think about everything Miss Applebaum had said. And done. Everything that we could remember. The more we thought, the more amazed we were by her. Even in death, she was shocking. Original. She had planned so much. She had chosen so well.

Miss Applebaum, Henry, and Zelda. We would be bound even closer now. Henry with his hawk eyes and fear of falling air conditioners. Zelda with her long hair and terror of the end of living.

We waited until the Channel 4 eleven-o'clock news was over. Most of the pet walkers in the building had finished their evening strolls by then. The elevator in the hallway was silent. It would be safest now.

We put the raccoon coat on Miss Applebaum, and Henry lifted her gently into the wheelchair. We carefully picked everything we felt she would want to have with her. Her homburg hat. The tweed suit. Her school briefcase. The faded photograph of Miss Applebaum and her sailor. A flower blossom. A leaf. Henry gave her a button from his sleeve. I gave her a small lock of my hair. We wanted to do some things the way the ancient Egyptians did. By midnight, if anyone had come to a window in the Dakota, all they would have seen was a boy and girl pushing an old lady in a wheelchair into the shadows of the park.

We pushed Miss Applebaum through Strawberry Fields, and by the Angel of the Waters. We stayed as close to the circles of light from the lampposts as we dared but were always ready to disappear if we saw a patrol car. Miss Applebaum had spoken to us of many things. Of puzzles and mazes. Of the secret of the nine dots that she had told us was the secret of life itself. "The true answers are always beyond our expectations," we remembered Miss Applebaum telling us from the very beginning. We passed the lifeless form of the carousel and took Miss Applebaum past Shakespeare and Columbus and Madame Curie. All the statues were dark silhouettes against a half-moon sky, but we knew Miss Applebaum loved them. Ahead on the knoll would be her bench. "This bench!" she had cried. "This spot! This is the most wondrous place in the world! From here, you can see everything beautiful! This is where all civilization comes together and *means* something! Where it means something important! Profound!" we could hear her proclaiming. "The best of all the spirit of the world that has ever existed triumphs here and lives on!" she had sung.

Here we stopped at the edge of the trench. Together we lifted Miss Applebaum's body out of the wheelchair and laid her gently into what would be her grave.

Gently.

We covered her with enough earth so when the men would come with their machines they wouldn't see her. They would simply finish their job of filling the long, long trench.

We rolled the empty wheelchair out of the park. The snow would fall. Winter would come and go. And in the spring, the park would come alive again. The bulldozers and the trench would be gone. The bench would sit on a soft grassy hill once more. Children would come back to play and there would be the sounds of people and music. On such a beautiful day, we would return again and bring a begonia for Miss Applebaum.